He Went With

Champlain

Publisher's Note

He Went With Champlain was written over 60 years ago and tells the story of a young man accompanying Champlain on his adventures around the world.

An excellent storyteller, Louise Andrews Kent provides the reader with the opportunity to experience a different time and place through the eyes of the main character, including the social customs, religious beliefs, and racial relations. Taking place over 400 years ago, many parts of life are foreign and sometimes offensive to us now, including specific customs, practices, beliefs, and words. To maintain and provide historical accuracy and to allow a true representation of this time period the words used and the customs and attitudes described have not been removed or edited.

This edition published 2022
by Living Book Press

ISBN: 978-1-922919-03-8 (hardcover)
         978-1-922919-02-1 (softcover)

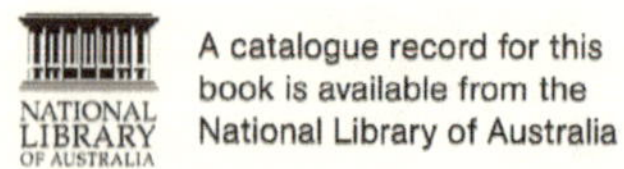

A catalogue record for this book is available from the National Library of Australia

He Went With Champlain

LOUISE ANDREWS KENT

ILLUSTRATED BY
ANTHONY D'ADAMO

Living Book Press

THE *He Went With...* SERIES

by

LOUISE ANDREWS KENT

Hannibal   Marco Polo   Christopher Columbus   Vasco da Gama

Magellan   Drake   Champlain   John Paul Jones

For more information about these, and other great books visit
www.livingbookpress.com/hewentwith/

CONTENTS

L. Superior
L. Huron
L. Michigan
L. Erie
A. D'Adamo

St. Lawrence R.
Quebec
Montreal
Port Royal
Acadia
L. Champlain
L. Ontario
Atlantic Ocean

CHAPTER 1

MEETING IN FRANCE

Tom Lee ran along a busy French wharf in Havre de Grace. He was a small, quick-moving boy, so small that he slipped through spaces that seemed too narrow for anything wider than a squirrel, so quick that the sun flashed on his silvery-blond hair as if he were in several places at once. He dodged past rolling casks of butter and cheese, dashed under a door carried by two tall men, darted past another pair who were lugging a stack of diamond-paned windows, jumped over a heap of sacks filled with peas.

Little peas, Tom thought, to plant in Canada. Lucky little peas! Then he smelled fish. He heard a loud miaow. A white cat pushed her head out of a bag slung across Tom's shoulder. Her head was about at the level of his belt as she looked out at a basket full of shining fish.

"It's not our fish, Minette," said Tom, patting her head.

Minette twitched her pink ears and yawned, showing an even pinker tongue. She purred politely for a moment and shut her green and yellow eyes. She knew that Tom would give her the fish when he had some. He always shared whatever he had with her. Lately they had both been hungry a good deal of the time.

Tom was moving more slowly now. He knew that if he were going to get on board Captain Pontgravé's ship and speak to the Sieur Samuel de Champlain, he must be careful. Etienne Brulé and Nicholas Marsolet had laughed at him and told him that he would never get on a ship bound for Canada. Especially not on Captain Pontgravé's ship.

"He'd eat two English goslings like you for his supper," Etienne had said, twisting his thin lips scornfully. "He wants only French in his crew."

"I'm half French," Tom Lee had said. "You know that. And France is my country."

"Half French—what good is that?" drawled Nicholas. "He'll take us to Canada—not you."

Etienne began dancing around Tom, saying, "We'll see rivers as wide as the ocean, waterfalls like mountains, mountains shining with gold and diamonds. We'll buy beaver skins for a string of beads and sell them in Paris for gold pieces. We'll see the Indians dance. We'll shoot deer and eat venison for our supper."

He stopped, out of breath, and Nicholas went on: "And you and your white cat will see nothing more strange than the coast of England and then the coast of France. Back and forth, carry wine to England, carry wool to France. Or have no ship at all. Plant cabbages. Kill a rabbit for supper and find yourself in prison while we are eating venison pie like dukes."

Just then a sailor had ordered Etienne and Nicholas to move

some casks. Nicholas had narrowed his pale blue eyes and had said, "I'll bet you the first beaver skin I get that you'll never get to Canada. Never get on the ship even."

"And don't let me catch you trying. I eat goslings," Etienne had said. The two braggarts swaggered off laughing.

Tom Lee had stood looking up at the ship. Gulls were sailing above it. They sounded like Minette when she mewed for fish. Through the cabin window Tom could see a man sitting at a table. The table was covered with books, papers, paints and brushes, pens and ink. The man was the Sieur de Champlain. Everyone on the wharf knew him. He was a famous man along the wharves of many French ports. He had sailed to the West Indies and visited Mexico. He had been to Canada and sailed up the St. Lawrence. He had fought for King Henry IV in the wars. The King had given him a pension and a place at court. Lately he had made him Royal Cartographer and Geographer. Another old soldier of the King's, the Sieur de Monts, was going to Canada to explore and found a colony. Champlain was going with the expedition. He would draw maps and find gold mines and look for a northwest passage to the great ocean on the other side of America. And whoever went with him would see wonderful things!

Tom had never seen the King but he had seen his picture. He thought the Sieur de Champlain looked a little like it. His brown hair was brushed up from his sunburned forehead. His horsechestnut-colored beard was trimmed like the King's. He was dressed in brown, the color of his beard, with a starched white ruff and sleeves puffed at the shoulders. His great beaver hat with the shining buckle and bunch of pheasant's feathers

lay on the table beside him. He was writing. The feather of his pen twisted fast through the air.

Tom saw Etienne and Nicholas, each with a cask on his shoulder, go below into the hold.

Now, Tom thought, I can get aboard. Only there are too many people on deck. The best way will be to climb to the masthead of that next ship there. The yards are almost touching. I'll cross over, drop to the deck when I see a good chance... get to the cabin before Etienne and Nicholas see me.

He was already doing it as fast as he thought.

The Sieur de Champlain looked up from the map he was lettering and glanced out of the cabin window. His eye caught the flash of sunlight on a small boy's blond head and on something white near his belt. It looked like a cat's head. Champlain watched with interest the boy's progress up to the yardarm. Every motion he made was the right one.

Champlain liked to see people move with purpose and decision. He himself was a lightly built man, wiry, able to sit quiet in thought but quick and decisive when the time came to move. The roof of the cabin soon cut off his view of the climbing boy and he went back to his lettering. He had forgotten all about the boy when, a few minutes later, there was a light firm tap on the cabin door.

"Come in," Champlain called, laying down his pen.

The door opened. The boy he had been watching stood there, a pink-cheeked, blue-eyed small boy, twelve years old, perhaps, Champlain thought. He seemed somewhat out of breath, but he stood straight and looked straight at you. The cat, Champlain noticed, was looking at him too. Or perhaps at the half-eaten plate of fish that he had forgotten and pushed aside.

"I can do something for you?" Champlain asked. He did not smile but his deep voice was kind as he added: "Perhaps you will tell me your name and where you come from—besides down the mast from the sky."

Tom bowed.

Champlain was pleased with the bow. There was no grace, no flourishing elegance about it but no stumbling clumsiness either. The boy put his hand properly over his heart, not over his stomach like a peasant. He spoke clearly too and his accent reminded Champlain of Brouage, where he was born. He thought of an old house with stone arches and a hall with beams of dark oak, of the Brouage marshes where salt used to be made, of apple orchards pink and white in spring sunshine.

"My name is Thomas Godfrey Lee," the boy was saying. "My father, an Englishman, was captain and owner of a barque that carried salt from Brouage to England. My mother was Anne Tremblay of Brouage."

Champlain moved slightly in his chair but he did not interrupt. It was his way to give his whole attention, to say nothing until the speaker had finished what he had to say.

"I went to school in Brouage," Tom went on. "I was taught by the Recollets, the Franciscan fathers there. I learned to read and write French, also a little Latin. My mother often crossed to England with my father. Three years ago their ship was lost in a great storm. The mate, a cousin of my father's, clung to a floating spar and was picked up by a French ship the next day. He was a kind man and he did his best for me. When he became mate of another cross-channel ship, he asked the Captain to take me as a cabin boy and I have been going back and forth across the Channel ever since. Dieppe is usually our French port. I have been useful, I think, because I speak both French and English. My cousin used to say that I would be a mate someday, perhaps even have a ship of my own, but he died last month of a fever. The Captain would have kept me on but I would like to see something more of the world than the coast of England and the coast of France. Besides," Tom added, "the Captain would not let me take Minette again. He says there are too many white cats on the ship already. Would you take us with you, sir, to Canada? Minette is a very good mouser."

Champlain said gently, "I am sorry about your parents. I never knew your father but I remember your mother well. Such a pretty girl and a cousin of mine, I think. In Brouage we were all cousins, more or less. Anne Tremblay—yes, a cousin of my mother's. I remember."

"She used to tell me about you, sir. Of how you fought for the King and of your journeys across the sea. How you painted pictures of Indians in Mexico and wrote books. They are very proud of you in Brouage."

"I would like to do something to deserve it," Champlain said quietly. "Perhaps some day I can. Now I would like you to answer a question."

"I'll try, sir."

Champlain moved his hat. It was a very grand hat, Tom noticed. He knew that a beaver hat was so valuable that when a man made his will, he would state which of his sons should inherit his hat. Monsieur de Champlain's hat was quite new.

Perhaps he had brought the skins for it from Canada himself. There was a book under the hat. Champlain opened it and began to read aloud from it.

Men travel—the author said—for many reasons. They are restless. They are criminals running away from punishment. They are poor and think it will be easier to get a living in a new land. They are greedy and expect to find gold and diamonds and swagger home in fine clothes. Some have a holy mission. They go to carry the cross among the savages. Others want power and think they can get it where the natives are wild and ignorant.

"What do you think of these reasons?" Champlain asked. "Is any of them yours?"

"No, sir. All I want is just to know, just to see what is there, on the other side of the world."

"Then, Thomas Godfrey Lee, my cousin who speaks two tongues—and a little Latin besides—you shall go with me to Canada—you and Minette. You shall learn to speak the language of the Indians and tell me what they say. You shall speak to them for me. I could never twist my tongue to a new speech and it is too late for me to learn now. You shall help me make a colony where the priests will come and bring Christianity to those poor savages. We'll win a new empire for France and find a passage through great lakes and rivers to the waters of the South Sea, the Pacific, as some call it. You shall learn to drive an Indian canoe through white water and track the moose in deep snow. You shall carry the French tongue far into deep forests. You shall be my servant and I will be your friend."

He must have seen that Tom could not speak because he

added, smiling: "Minette shall be the mother of many kittens who will purr with a Canadian accent. And now let's give her what's left of my dinner. I see she is looking at it with interest. And you, my cousin, Thomas Godfrey, shall go to the galley and ask the cook for some hot fish and good French bread and whatever else he has. Say I sent you. Do I speak your name right? Of course not. How should I—since it's English."

"I like the way you say it," Tom said.

He went off to the galley with Champlain's deep voice saying "Tom-a Go-de-froy" still sounding in his ears like a great bell chiming.

Nicholas Marsolet was being chased out of the galley by the cook. He ran into Tom and nearly knocked him over.

"Out of my way, gosling!" Nicholas said, scowling so that under his dark brows his eyes were only blue slits in his fat white face. "What are you doing on this ship?" he added as Tom dodged briskly around a coil of rope. "Perhaps you'd like a swim in the harbor."

"I've just come for the beaver skin you owe me," Tom said, slipping neatly out of Nicholas' reach. "And to take an order to the cook from my master."

"And who's your master?"

Nicholas' voice was changing and it squeaked like a rusty hinge.

"My cousin, the Sieur Samuel de Champlain of Brouage," Tom answered. He bowed politely and stepped quickly into the galley, leaving Nicholas with his mouth hanging open, showing his crooked teeth. They always made Tom think of the fangs of an old wolf that he had found dead near the church at Brouage one cold winter.

Minette had licked Champlain's plate clean and was sitting on his lap purring her thanks. She jumped down when Tom came into the cabin and made figure eights between his feet, caressing his legs with her tail, purring louder than ever.

"*Ron, ron, ron,*" she said, and Tom answered, "*Ron, ron, ron, petit patapon,*" for since Minette was a French cat, they naturally spoke French to each other.

Minette then carefully washed her already clean paws. They looked like sea shells underneath and above like dandelion fluff. She also did her face and ears and hind legs. When she had finished and was humping her back, making a white marble arch of herself, Tom held out her bag. She got into it and turned around, purring, while Tom fastened the strap that went around her neck.

Champlain said, "Why, she is like an Indian baby. They are strapped to little boards and ride on their mothers' backs. See—like this."

He found his box of colors, took up his brush, dipped it in water and started painting. In a few moments it was all there— the black-haired, brown-faced papoose wrapped in a beaver robe, the board with its corners trimmed with bright beads and colored porcupine quills, the mother in her deerskins.

"And I shall see them like that?" Tom said.

"Yes. Only sometimes the mother takes the board off her back and props it against something, papoose and all. You go into an Indian cabin and you may find a row of babies looking at you out of their black eyes. You'd think they were dolls. They don't wink. Here, take the picture if you would like it."

"Thank you, sir. I will keep it, always."

He went towards the door, turned and made another of his quick bows.

"Where are you going?" Champlain asked. "You must sleep on board. We sail tomorrow if the wind is fair."

"I have been living with a farmer's family since I left my cousin's ship, working for my food and lodging. I still owe them some hours of pulling weeds out of the cabbage patch. If I never saw another cabbage, it would be such a pleasure."

Champlain laughed. "You are right to pay your debt but wrong about cabbages. We'll need to plant them in Canada. We must have French gardens there. And Canadian weeds are twice as tall as weeds here."

"It will be a pleasure to pull them out of your garden, sir," Tom Lee said.

FRENCHMAN'S BAY

Iᴛ ᴡᴀs Mᴀʀᴄʜ 7th, 1604, when Captain Pontgravé's ship sailed from Le Havre. The sailors who had made the voyage before called it a bad one. They met great mountains of ice and drifting fields of ice twenty miles long. The wind failed. Etienne Brulé told Tom that if it did not blow them out of the fog and ice the next day, the youngest boy on the ship would be flogged.

"That is how they pray for wind in this part of the world," Etienne added with his twisting smile.

Tom, who knew very well who the youngest boy on the ship was, half believed him but he had no chance to find out if the story was true. The wind sprang up. It was only a light breeze but it blew the fog away and the sun shone. The sailors sang and danced on the deck.

Captain Pontgravé saw another ship making its way among the ice fields. He greeted it by roaring out, "Malouins!" This meant men of St. Malo. Captain Pontgravé came from St. Malo and the greatest compliment he could pay you was to shout "Malouins!" to you.

When Pontgravé heard the Captain answer and found out that he was really from St. Malo, he slapped Tom joyfully on the back and sent him to the cabin to set out glasses and a jug of apple cider. This was the nearest Tom came to being flogged.

He was back on deck in time to hear a strange hoarse roar, far louder than the Captain's big voice. It was a great white whale, spouting near the ship. It came steaming fast through the green water, straight at them, as if an iceberg had suddenly come to life and was angry at them.

Perhaps it thinks we are a whale with sails and it's going to fight us, Tom thought.

However, the whale only turned a surprised little eye towards the ship and suddenly vanished below the waves. The May night was short but it seemed long because the hoarse spouting of whales never seemed to stop. In the morning the wind dropped again but they were in sunny blue water away from the ice.

"Was it like this when you sailed to Canada before, sir?" Tom asked Champlain.

He had found out that if he talked to his master at mealtimes, Champlain would eat his food instead of forgetting it while he worked on his charts. Tom was pleased to see that Champlain did not look so thin as he did when the voyage began.

"Much the same," he said in answer to Tom's question. "Fog, ice, gales."

He showed Tom a paper he had, ruled into columns with dates and the names of places, a sort of timetable.

"See," he said. "We left Honfleur on May 27th."

Tom looked at the paper. Honfleur was the only familiar place. The other names—the Grand Banks, Ile Percée, Gaspe,

Tadoussac, Quebec, Mount Royal, La Chine Rapids—were all strange and made chills of excitement run up and down his spine.

"It won't be long now," his master was saying, "before we see great clouds of sea birds. There are islands where they huddle so thick that you cannot move without stepping on their eggs. The sailors knock them over with clubs, poor things. Some birds are so greedy that you can catch them in the air. You bait a hook with a herring and swing it towards a bird. He snatches it and you snatch him by the leg as he swoops."

"I'd like to see that," Tom said.

"Oh, you'll see it and six-foot salmon and swordfish leaping and plunging their swords into the backs of whales. You'll see the saddleback seals."

"Is that the one Nicholas says he can ride like a horse?" Tom asked.

"That is something *I'd* like to see," said Champlain with a twinkle in his brown eyes.

"It was a morning like this one when we first sailed up the St. Lawrence," he added. "The fog burned off and we saw high rocky hills towering over us. We were soon at Tadoussac near the mouth of the Saguenay River. There were fires on shore and birch-bark canoes pulled up on the beach with their naked owners beside them, looking half roasted by the sun."

He went on to tell how the Indians had their faces painted. Some had blue noses, black bands across their eyebrows and scarlet cheeks. Others had stripes of red, black and blue from ears to mouth or a single wide black stripe around the eyes.

"We had two Indians of this tribe with us," Champlain

said. "We call them Montagnais. They had visited our King in Paris and they had told their friends that he had promised to help them against their enemies, who are called the Iroquois. Eighty of these painted warriors listened in silence. Then they passed us pipes of tobacco and we smoked with them. This is a sign of friendship; not one I am fond of, but the Indians can go without food for days if they have tobacco."

He went on to say that after the smoking was over, the Indians invited the French to a great feast. They were celebrating a victory over the Iroquois. There were ten kettles, each on a separate fire, with meat of moose, bear, beaver and wild ducks and geese. Each guest was given a porringer made of birch bark. The plump olive-skinned Indian women filled the porringers from the kettles.

Dogs leaped around the kettles and the Indians wiped their hands on them.

"They make better napkins than you might think," Champlain said, smiling.

There was a dance after the feast. The warriors took the scalps of their enemies in their hands and danced up and down in one place, beating their hands together, shaking gourds or skin drums with pebbles in them, panting like men out of breath and crying, "Ho! Ho! Ho!" Their songs were so grave and monotonous that, Champlain said, it was a relief when they burst into shrieks and howls. The women danced too, sometimes throwing off their beaver robes and dancing in the ice-cold water. They got into canoes and splashed each other with paddles. Their children splashed too and danced beside the tall painted warriors.

After the *tabagie*, which is their name for a feast, they spent many days in polite talk and in trading furs with the French. Champlain made a trip up the Saguenay and found it—he told Tom—a most unpleasant country, deserted and unfit for animals or birds.

His master, Tom noticed, never spoke well of any place that did not have rich meadows where crops could be raised. The great forests of spruce and pine he found dark and gloomy. He cared nothing for the way a hemlock would find room for its roots on what looked like a bare rock. He carried always with him his French love of gardens. The trees he admired were French trees, twisty-armed oaks or silvery beeches.

He liked an island near Quebec, he told Tom, where wild grapes grew and where there were the meadows he was always looking for. It split the St. Lawrence in two for twenty miles. Across from it on the northwestern side of the river was a tower of white water falling over a high cliff. The water in the pool below rose in steam so that you might think a kettle was boiling. Above the island the river narrowed suddenly. On the southeastern side was beautiful country with vines and blossoming fruit trees. On the north rose a great gray rock. There was an Indian village at the foot of it. Stadaconna was one Indian name for it, though other Indians called it Quebec.

"I dreamed of it last night," Champlain said, "dreamed that I would win it in peace and lose it in war, that I would feel, when I saw that old gray rock against the sky, that I had come home. In my dream someone told me that I would fail in most of my dreams for it and that I would die there, but they told me too that there would be gardens there and high church towers and flags with the lilies of France and that the French tongue would still be heard in its narrow, twisting streets for hundreds of years."

Then he added: "But it was only a dream, that city on the rock with the morning sun shining on its towers. The Sieur de Monts had decided that we should make our colony in a milder climate and in some place more easily defended against the Indians than Quebec. Though I can see how a few cannon properly placed—well, I talk too much."

Tom wished his master would talk more. He always thought of Champlain as his master and liked to hear him say, "My servant Thomas." It was an honor to be called servant by such a man.

He was disappointed that he was not to see Quebec, but then all the country was strange and new. They saw the vast flocks of sea birds, seals plunging through the water. Nicholas decided not to ride a seal after all, though he had bet Tom another beaver skin that he would. Nicholas owed a good many imaginary beaver skins to various members of the crew.

Tom was not worrying about imaginary beaver skins but about Minette who had suddenly disappeared. She had enjoyed the voyage and had won much praise for her skill in catching mice. She had even brought rats on deck a few times, though usually she left that part of the day's work to the ship's cat. He was an enormous black tom, a patronizing-looking cat who would sit sleepily on a coil of rope in the sunshine while Minette frisked around him. By moonlight he would sometimes circle around her on the deck, uttering weird growls and shrieks.

Minette was a great favorite of the sailors, who caught fish for her when the ship was becalmed and who gave her scraps off their plates on stormy days. She had been on deck in all kinds of weather but she had always found time to visit the cabin. The last time Tom had seen her, she was sitting on Champlain's lap while he was writing his account of the voyage.

Tom hunted for her all over the ship. They were in sight of land now and might soon find a place for their colony. He wanted to be sure to take Minette along when he landed. There had been waves the night before that sprayed over the deck. Could Minette have been washed overboard? She did not come when he called.

"She's all right," a sailor told him kindly. "Just now she was outside the galley eating a fine chunk of a salmon I caught."

"I met her in the forecastle," one of the carpenters told him. "She rubbed against my legs and purred as pretty as you please."

So Tom went back to his work. They were exploring bays and rivers and islands. The sailors were heaving the lead, a triangular block of metal greased with butter or lard, to find out the depth of the water. Sand and shells would stick to it when it touched bottom so they could also find out what the bottom was like. Tom was helping his master record what they found on the charts that Champlain was always making—charts that would keep ships off rocks and sandbanks for many years.

At last they came to Passamaquoddy Bay and sailed up a broad stream. Misty mountains rose in the north. The river ran peacefully past fertile shores. They began to see land birds instead of gulls. They called the river the St. Croix and an island twelve miles upstream St. Croix Island.

On the east the island rose steeply fifty feet above the rushing tide. The western shore was a gentle slope. There were trees that could be used for building and clay for brickmaking. The soil looked good for gardens. It would be a convenient place for meeting Indian fur traders, the Sieur de Monts said, and it could be easily fortified if the Indians proved hostile. Since it was south of Quebec the climate would be milder, he said.

The day they landed and began unloading the ship was warm and beautiful. There were black birds with red and yellow shoulder patches flying and wheeling as precisely as a well-drilled troop of soldiers. Brown rabbits stared at the ship in surprise and scuttered back into the bushes. A big hawk dived into the water and came up with a fish in his claws. An even bigger eagle with a shining white head chased the hawk and made him drop the fish on shore. Then he settled down to eat his dinner comfortably on a sun-baked rock while the hawk went off screaming.

Tom was with his master who was helping the Sieur de Monts make a plan for their habitation, as they called the group of houses that would be built for the colony. Champlain was sitting on a rock, drawing with his usual swiftness and neatness an outline of the island and of the river shores. He began by decorating it with a compass rose and a French lily pointing north. Tom, under de Monts' direction, began driving stakes into the ground for the corners of the storehouse.

Before long Champlain needed more paper. Tom went back to the ship to get it. The tide was high, so high that the ship could come in close to the shore. The sailors had laid planks from the gangway to a high flat rock. With Captain Pontgravé roaring at them, they were rolling casks to the shore. The casks stopped rolling just as Tom came out of the spruce trees near the rock. He heard Pontgravé and the sailors laughing. He soon saw why.

On the planks was a slow-moving procession. In front was Minette, looking back over her shoulder and mewing at intervals. Behind her, tails straight in the air, with faces as innocent as apple blossoms, falling over paws too big for them, came five plump, fluffy kittens. Two were white, one was white spotted with black, one was black with a white nose and paws and one was black without a white hair. One of the first families of North America had arrived.

It was a long time before there was another family of settlers in New France. The colonists who came with the Sieur de Monts were not farmers. It was not easy to get a French peasant to leave his farm and settle in an unknown wilderness. There were carpenters, masons, soldiers, a surgeon, and a priest, Father Aubry.

Everyone got to work to help build the habitation. Though they were so bitten by black flies and mosquitoes they could hardly see, they built a storehouse fifty feet long, houses for de Monts and for Champlain, a chapel, a house for the priest, others for the laborers and the soldiers. They also built a kitchen, a forge for making ironwork, and a mill where grain was ground by hand.

The doors and windows, which Tom had seen being loaded on the ship at Le Havre, were now set in place. There were benches and tables too from France. Before long there were French gardens in New France. Each man had a plot of land.

Even Tom had a piece of land of his own where he sowed peas and beans and even cabbages.

By September the habitation was built. Pontgravé sailed back to France. He left a seventeen-ton pinnace for Champlain's use. In this little ship, on September 2nd, Champlain started to explore the coast south of St. Croix. He took soundings, drew charts of rivers, bays and peninsulas, marked rocks and out-lined mountains as they loomed out of the fog. They rounded point after point, finding sandbanks, dangerous ledges, pleas-ant harbors. Once the pinnace struck a reef but they got her ashore in time and mended the hole in her side.

They were in a great bay where the rocky islands were all covered with pointed firs.

"They look like porcupines," said Tom, who had seen these prickly animals on the shore across from St. Croix Island. Minette had seen one too and had made too close an acquain-tance with it. Tom had had to pull two quills out of her nose.

The largest of these porcupine islands had tall purple-brown cliffs on the ocean side.

"There must be iron in them," Champlain said, and Tom asked, "Shall we call it Iron Bound then?" His master nodded. Tom wrote the name down on the chart he was marking. He wanted to call the bay after his master, but Champlain shook his head and wrote St. Sauviur on his chart. Tom however wrote down Frenchman's Bay on his.

There was fog hanging over the bay that morning but it burned off by noon. Then they saw that what they had thought was only another wooded island, bigger and higher than the others, was really a massive mountain. There were trees on its lower slopes but the tops of its several heights, some pointed, some domed, were bare and rocky. All were wild and lonely.

To Champlain with his love of open, smiling meadows it was only another expanse of grim rock. He marked it on his chart as Mount Desert.

"It's a dreary place," he said to Tom.

"Worse than Quebec?" Tom asked.

"Why, no! And you would like to know why then do I dream of a city at Quebec and none here? It sounds foolish perhaps but I feel sure in my heart that only from a settlement on the St. Lawrence shall I find a northern passage to the Pacific."

He was drawing a map of the world as he spoke.

"See now," he said. "To reach China from France, whether we go east or west, we must sail through a hot climate, reach a cold one, be tossed about by fierce gales, sail back into burning heat and then find our way north again. This is hard on both ships and sailors. Now when I journeyed to the West Indies and Mexico I saw an isthmus—you know what that is?"

"Yes, sir. A narrow neck of land. One of your charts shows one between North and South America. Was that it?"

"Right—the Isthmus of Panama. Well, I said then and still say that men could dig a canal through it so ships could be saved those weary journeys around Cape Horn. The Spaniards laughed at me but I still think it could be done. Only to find a passage would be better for France."

"A northwest passage, sir?"

"If that is the only way, yes, but since surely it would be ice-bound much of the year, I hope we can find one farther south," Champlain said. "From what the Indians tell me of the St. Lawrence and the lakes beyond, it may be there. But we'll talk more of that when we are not taking soundings or we'll have another hole in our side. How many fathoms there?"

It was on the next day that they sailed around Iron Bound Island. Champlain found its latitude with his bronze astrolabe. It was made in 1603 and had the date on it. He told Tom what the latitude was. When they were on the cliff side of the island, Tom asked Etienne and Nicholas whether they could see land to the east.

"Except that little rocky gray island a few miles away I can't see any," Tom added. "If your eyes are really keen you might see it. Mine aren't good enough."

"I see it. I see land," Nicholas Marsolet said, shading his blue eyes. "It's very faint but darker than the sea—a long low coast."

"I see it too," Etienne said, "but it isn't all low. There's a snow-capped mountain in the middle of it."

"You both have remarkable eyesight," Tom said. "The next land out there is Portugal."

Champlain, who had been listening, laughed till the cliffs echoed. This was almost certainly the first time that this joke was ever made in Frenchman's Bay. By evening Tom wished he had not made it.

They went on shore to hunt for berries and wild mushrooms and to get mussels to put in a fish stew. Champlain found mushrooms in the woods and he showed Tom which ones were good to eat. He said the bright orange ones, like little parasols with white freckles, were poison but the dull orange-brown ones, spongy green underneath, were good eating. When he last saw Tom, he was filling a basket with them.

Champlain went back to the ship and worked on his charts. The mussel-gathering party soon had filled a bushel basket with the blue-black shellfish. The berry pickers found blackberries and sour little mountain cranberries. The pinnace sailed west towards the head of the bay. Champlain, seeing Nicholas pass by the cabin door, asked, "Have you seen Thomas?"

"He went below looking for Minette the last time I saw him," Nicholas said. "He was going to feed her and the kittens."

This was strictly true except that it happened before noon. It was now almost sunset. Actually, as Nicholas and Etienne both knew, Tom was still on Iron Bound Island.

Tom never became very fond of mushrooms or of cranberries either, or of mussels. During his visit to Iron Bound Island, they were all he had to eat. All three kinds of food are better if cooked. Tom had no flint and steel for making a fire. He had not yet learned the Indian way of spinning one piece of wood against another until a spark came.

He stayed close to the cove where they had landed, hoping to see the pinnace coming across the blue and white water of the bay but there was only the dark bulk of Mount Desert, the pale blue hills to the north of the bay and the prickly-looking islands, some edged with brown rock, some with pinkish yellow. In the afternoon fog began to drift in from the east and the breeze dropped.

Night is coming, Tom thought with a shiver.

He knew the pinnace could never sail back in that gray stillness. He had a small hatchet tucked into his belt. Champlain had given this one to Tom, telling him that he could use it in trade for beaver skins when they met some friendly Indians.

An Indian would make a shelter with it, Tom thought.

There were small balsam trees growing near the cove. He cut down two, lopped off their branches and leaned the poles against a third tree. He thatched his shelter with branches he had cut off, with others he made a bed on the floor and he cut some for blankets. He stuffed Minette's bag with balsam needles for a pillow.

His balsam tent would have made an Indian laugh. A good breeze would have blown it down in a minute. Still it was better than sleeping on a bare rock in the fog, which was now so thick that Tom could hear it dripping off the trees.

It was what is called a quiet night; that is, a night on which every sound can be distinctly heard. In his prickly nest, Tom could hear every ripple of the tide wearing small pebbles into sand, smoothing rough ones into ovals, grinding shells, giving drinks to thirsty barnacles. He heard night herons going *quonk* near the marshy pond back of the beach and seals barking in another cove far across the island.

He could hear field mice squeaking and scampering in the long grass. One ran over his foot and he wished for Minette and her family. He wondered if they were happy.

For a long time he could not sleep. He tried saying over some of the Indian words he knew. On the pinnace he had made friends with one of the Indian guides and had learned to speak his language a little. The Indians, he noticed, were learning French faster than he was picking up the guide's language. Most of the Frenchmen did not try very hard to learn but were content with a mixture of French and Indian words. They called this mixture *baragouin*. When they spoke it they were satisfied that they were speaking the Indian language. The Indians, of course, felt sure that they were speaking good French.

Tom wished his favorite Indian, whose long name meant the Trout, were there to talk to him. He even would have been glad to see Nicholas Marsolet walk out of the dark fog.

He would have said that he never slept at all on his spicy pillow and yet suddenly it was morning and crows were scolding among the spruces across the cove. The fog was burning off, leaving only a hot haze on the hills. The bay was a pale silky blue. Hardly a breath of air moved it. There was no sign of the pinnace.

"She couldn't sail anyway in this calm," Tom told himself.

He ate blackberries for breakfast and a mushroom made almost lukewarm by being cut in pieces and left on a rock in the sun. He tried to eat a second one but decided that enough is plenty. He had mussels for dinner. Sea gulls were getting mussels too. Tom opened his with a knife, but the gulls flew high up into the blue September air and dropped their mussels on the rocks. Then, mewing, they swooped down and ate them unless some friend or relation got there first. They also caught pollack. They were welcome to all the pollack in the bay so far as Tom was concerned—pollack was an uninteresting fish even when cooked.

He had found, the day before, a cold spring bubbling out of

the grass in a meadow above the cove. He went back to it and drank out of his hands, which were well coated with balsam pitch and stained with blackberries and cranberries. The tide covered the mussel beds that noon so he ate another lukewarm mushroom and some sour cranberries. When the tide went down he had some more mussels.

After eating them, he walked eastward along the shore, hoping that he might see the pinnace, but the bay was empty.

Long swim to Portugal, he thought, managing a smile.

The waves were stirring gently in a cove facing south. Beyond it a high gray rock, like the head of some ancient giant, rose out of swirling green water. The tide was ebbing, leaving rocks covered with red-brown seaweed and barnacles. Tom made his way down to the edge of the sea and walked through the slippery seaweed to the foot of the rock.

Now he could see that a small channel ran back into a cave. He could walk in on the rocks that edged it. The sea rose and fell and echoed in the cave. Sea anemones opened and shut their pale fingers in a small pool. Limpets clung to the rock. Tom pried up several with his knife, ate the contents and set the shells floating like boats in the pool. He could see his face in the pool—the pitch on it, the cranberry stains, the balsam needles in his hair.

Outside the sun was hot on the rocks. He lay down, just for a moment, he told himself, to rest and look up at the sun. It was moving fast towards the west. Sleep fell on him, gently, like the wind moving in the pointed firs.

CHAPTER 3

ST. CROIX

THE PINNACE had sailed a long distance up the bay before Champlain, working on his charts, remembered that he had eaten no supper. He was about to call for Tom when Etienne came running to the cabin with the news that there was a fire on shore and Indians dancing around it.

The Indians were shy at first but after the Trout had talked to them they became friendly. They gave the Frenchmen fish from their kettles to eat. They promised to show Champlain the passage around the island and a great river farther south called the Penobscot. Not until the next morning did Champlain realize that Tom was missing.

It was not Champlain's way to scold people for their faults but rather to see that the results of their faults were undone. The Indians had guided them through the channel north of Mount Desert and into a quiet bay edged with wooded hills. The pinnace lay becalmed in this bay. There was not a breath of wind there, none in the great bay outside.

"Since we cannot sail back," Champlain said quietly to the

Trout, "we must send a boat or a canoe for him. Which will be the best?"

"Canoe faster," the Trout said.

"Tell the chief that if two of his men will go, they shall each have a hatchet."

"I will be one of the men," said the Trout.

On shore near the Indian camp, the Trout talked to the chief, then to a tall Indian with one cheek painted red and the other yellow striped with white.

"This man will go," the Trout said, "but he says he must have two hatchets, one for him, one for canoe. He says we must go swiftly, for before sunset the west wind will rise. The tide will run against it. There will be white water. I will go without pay. Tom is my friend."

"Go then," said Champlain, and the canoe was soon speeding down the channel.

Nicholas and Etienne thought it wise to keep out of the Sieur de Champlain's way. They had never seen him angry but they were not anxious to learn what his anger was like. They got into a boat that was starting to go back to the ship. They thought Champlain did not see them, so his voice coming across the water was an unpleasant surprise.

"I will see you, Etienne, and you, Nicholas, in my cabin as soon as I come back to the ship. Wait for me there."

They sat in glum silence for a while. Then Nicholas got out his dice and they began tossing them. They used French beads to keep score with. So many white beads were worth a blue bead, so many yellow beads were worth a red bead. A certain number of red beads were worth a knife and two knives were worth a beaver skin. Nicholas had soon lost two knives. He handed them over scowling and then said, "What shall we tell him?"

"Why, the truth," Etienne said, rattling his dice in their leather shaker. "We're a little tired of Tom Lee's airs. 'My master this, my master that... my master the Sieur de Champlain says...' You'd think he owned him. We thought it no harm for him to have a night on the island by himself. We didn't know we'd sail up here and get becalmed. It was a mistake. We're sorry."

He grinned and went on shaking the dice.

"You may say that if you're fool enough," Nicholas said, narrowing his pale blue eyes. "I knew nothing about it and shall say so."

"And leave me to take the blame!" Etienne said loudly. "You knew he was left behind as well as I did. You're a traitor and a coward."

They were fighting when Champlain reached the cabin door. He stood for a moment watching them wrestling in the small space between the table and his bunk.

Then he said quietly, "Nicholas and Etienne."

The wrestlers let go their holds and stumbled to their feet.

"I think I understand this matter," Champlain said. "Nicholas, when you are planning to lie, don't get mixed up with someone honest. Etienne, when you think of telling the truth, don't choose a companion who is, as you say, a coward and a traitor. And don't announce your plans so loudly. I am not in the habit of listening at doors but sound travels clearly over quiet water. Now—you may go below and stay there until the canoe comes back—if it comes back. The wind is rising and blowing against the tide. We shall sail out and try to shorten their journey. If Thomas returns safely, you may pay for the journey out of the hatchets you have for trade. If he does not, I will decide what your punishment will be. You may go."

In the cave that was the open mouth of the Great Head, the returning tide began to move the delicate fingers of the anemones. The bunches of brown grapes on the seaweed rose and fell. Sea urchins and barnacles drank the salty water. An enormous crimson and purple jellyfish was carried close to the rocks. Seals woke up in the cove beyond and barked to each other that it was time to go fishing. A wave, bigger than its companions, broke on the rocks below the cave. Its foam was blown spinning out towards Portugal. An eagle flew screaming over the bay but Tom Lee slept on.

In the sheltered cove that faced the bay, the bow of a birch-bark canoe grated gently on the pebbles. The Trout sprang out of it and ran to the balsam shelter but it was empty. The owner of the canoe lifted it out of the water and carried it on his head above high-water mark. He showed the Trout mushrooms scattered on the rocks, mussel shells farther on, cranberries floating in a little rock pool, a broken branch.

"That way," he said, pointing. "You run, find him. I sleep."

The Trout came in sight of Great Head just as a big wave dashed over a sunny rock west of the cave. It soaked Tom Lee's dark blue doublet, his blue camlet cloak with the red lining, his tumbled yellow hair. He got to his knees. Before he could stand another wave had soaked him again. He stood up, rubbing the salt out of his eyes. The first thing he saw was the Trout, a bronze figure, leaping from one purple-bronze rock to the next.

He waved to Tom to follow and turned again towards the northern cove, looking back from time to time to see if Tom was all right, clapping his hand to his mouth and yelling as loud as an eagle when he came in sight of the cove. By the time Tom reached it, both Indians were in the canoe, holding it steady with their paddles.

They laughed as they saw Tom run down over the pebbles.

"Sieur de Champlain send us," the Trout said. "You get in, lie down. Not move. White water coming. We go behind islands."

There were whitecaps out in the dark blue bay but behind the bristling porcupine islands the water was still calm. It was beginning to turn pink from the sunset clouds.

They had to cross open sea between the islands but the Indians managed the canoe so well that few waves broke into it. Still, Tom found himself lying in a good deal of water. In the lee of one of the islands, the Trout handed Tom a birch-bark porringer.

"You sit up now. Throw out water," the Trout said.

From then on, Tom was kept busy bailing. He was never to forget that evening—the sound of the waves striking the canoe and tossing it against the tide, the spindrift pink in the red sunset, the grunted orders of the painted Indian in the stern to the Trout in the bow, the moon's broken path over the tumbled bay, the pointed firs black against the moon, his arms tired from bailing.

Then suddenly the moonlight struck on something silver. It was the sails of the pinnace running towards them. She turned to come up into the wind. Tom could see a light in her cabin. He knew that his master was sitting there writing and waiting for him. To that master, who greeted him with kindness and without reproaches, Tom silently promised a life-long devotion.

Nicholas and Etienne handed over their hatchets the next morning, Nicholas sulkily, Etienne with his usual careless cheerfulness. Champlain saw to it that the Trout, who had asked for nothing, received not only a hatchet but plenty of beads and a French kettle besides. Tom gave his friend all his French beads and a fringed strip of red cloth. It was meant for a sash but the Trout immediately tied it around his head. This ornament was much admired along the Penobscot River. More than one fierce-looking warrior would have liked such a magnificent ornament but they had to be contented with their own bands of deerskin brightened with colored porcupine quills or with moose hair dyed red. The Trout was offered many beavers for his red cloth but he would not part with it.

In the country through which they traveled there were tales of a vast city with high towers and small dark-skinned inhabitants. Norumbega was its name. They were always moving towards it but it was always a little farther on. Perhaps this was because of its magicians who lived there and who could turn brick to gold and shell beads to diamonds.

Nicholas and Etienne, who both now understood the Indians well, told these stories. Tom, however, never heard anything more exciting from the inhabitants of the smoky bark cabins they visited than: "How many knives for a beaver?" The magic city melted into the golden leaves of the maples and diamonds of hoar frost on reeds and rushes.

They sailed along the coast as far south as the Kennebec. Since food was running short, they turned and ran northeast towards St. Croix. They arrived there on October 2nd, only a few days before snow began to fall.

Of that winter Tom never liked to speak. He lived through it. That was all he cared to remember. Winds, colder than any that ever blew down the channel between France and England, whistled through the walls of the hastily built houses. Their wine and cider froze and had to be served out by the pound. There were shellfish of several kinds on the shores of the island but to get them in raging snowstorms was almost impossible. Still, Tom did get them for his master and for himself. They both preferred them to the salt fish and meat brought from France.

There was little fuel to cook them. They had cut down most of the trees on the island to build the habitation. In summer it had been easy to cross to the mainland for wood and to go hunting. Now the eighteen-foot tides sent drifting ice cakes crashing between the island and the shore. It was often impossible to get across the river. However, there were always a few members of the colony who battled the wind, tide and ice to go hunting with the Indians of the mainland.

Champlain was one of these hunters. The Trout was another. Tom, Nicholas and Etienne were part of the hunting expeditions. The Indians lent them snowshoes and showed them how to track the moose. They would follow one of the big animals for days before it sank helplessly in a snowdrift and floundered there until they could kill it with their arrows and short spears.

Most of the settlers, however, preferred to huddle over a few coals in a brazier or to lie in their beds, talking about what they would eat when they got back to Paris and its good cooks. Many of these men had scurvy before the winter was over. They could hardly move because of the violent pains in their arms and legs, which were swollen and covered with purple-brown bruises. Their gums swelled too and their teeth fell out. Their coughs and groans could be heard all over the little settlement.

Tom tried to help the surgeon take care of them. He had helped the surgeon on the voyage to Canada and in the summer and winter when there were broken bones to set, wounds to sew up and boils to be opened with the lancet. It did no good to use the lancet to open the veins of men with scurvy. This was the only remedy the surgeon knew. With Tom's help he went through the ghastly business of dissecting some of the dead bodies before they were buried in the fast-growing cemetery. He learned nothing about the causes of the disease in this way but Tom did learn something about anatomy.

Before long the surgeon became ill himself. Of the seventy-eight men who spent that winter on St. Croix, he was one of thirty-five who died. The day before his death he handed Tom his leather case of surgical tools.

"This country," he said, between choking coughs, "cannot be made into an empire with fur traders alone. It will need surgeons too. Learn to use these tools, Tom. Learn for the sake of France."

Tom helped to bury him the next day.

In March some Indians came and traded fresh meat for knives and beads. The snow would melt soon, they told Tom.

But at the end of April it was still four feet deep in some places. The ice heaved and smashed in the river. Twenty of the settlers hovered near death with scurvy, but as the ice melted and the sun grew warm they began to get better. Champlain thought it was because they now had plenty of fresh shellfish and because the hunters could easily bring fresh meat across the channel. He thought too much salt food was the cause of the disease. The Indians, he figured, ate no salt and they did not have scurvy unless they ate the white man's food.

After the six months of winter were over came the fear that Pontgravé and his supply ships might have been lost at sea. They began to look for him in April but it was not until June 15th that Etienne's sharp eyes saw a shallop coming up the river with the tide. The ship had stayed downstream but in the shallop they could see Pontgravé's jolly red face. His great shout of "Malouins!" soon rang across the river and brought the colony to the shore.

There was great rejoicing but even Pontgravé looked sad when he heard about the winter. He agreed with the Sieur de Champlain that a better place must be found for the colony.

CHAPTER 4

PORT ROYAL

THE PARTY that went south along the coast on June 17th, 1605, consisted of the Sieur de Monts, Champlain, and a crew of twenty. An Indian called Panonias and his wife went as interpreters. They were of different tribes and spoke two Indian languages and some French. Tom missed the Trout, who had gone back to his own people, but Panonias and his wife were kind to him and he learned their languages.

The weather was fine and the winds favorable. The winter at St. Croix began to seem like a dark dream. Etienne's zither sounded gay as he played for the sailors to dance on the deck. They went up broad rivers with the tide, passed islands where wild grapes grew, saw wide beaches where the sand blazed like gold. Friendly Indians all along this coast danced when they saw the ship. Champlain gave them knives and they danced better than ever.

These Indians made gardens with wooden hoes and planted corn and beans and sun-flowers with roots that tasted like Jerusalem artichokes. These tribes lived in round wigwams thatched with reeds and surrounded by palisades. They had no furs to trade and the canoes in which they visited the ship were clumsy affairs. They made them by burning the insides of tree trunks, digging out the charred part with stone hatchets, then repeating the process until the trunk was hollow. The men were tall and fine-looking but treacherous, vengeful and great thieves.

At the moment they were full of friendliness. They loved music and were especially pleased when Etienne took his zither on shore and played for them. Twenty of the tallest braves danced in a ring, stamping and shouting *Lo, lo, lo, La, la, la.* If one broke out of the ring, they would cry out at him and strike him.

As it grew dark, they lighted fires. The dancing went on. Tom sat on a rock, the only one on the beach, watching the moving shadows on the sand and the firelight striking on the painted faces of the dancers. Their hair was shaved off in front. The back had feathers stuck in it. In the woods the day before, Tom had seen the bird from which the feathers came, a bird as tall as a small boy, with a spreading tail of bronze. His bright red throat swelled as he uttered an angry gobbling cry. They were good eating, Panonias told him.

Etienne had stuck a feather in his own black hair. The fire struck on his high cheekbones, on his nose like an osprey's beak, and on his thin smiling lips.

Why, he's an Indian himself, Tom thought.

Etienne was tired of playing now. As the music stopped, the Indians crowded around him, bringing him presents. They gave him tobacco and a pipe to smoke it in, a pipe of carved red sandstone. One Indian brought him a fawn's skin, soft and almost white. Another handed him the skin of a rattlesnake about six feet long, and the rattles, hung on a cord. Etienne promptly wrapped the girdle around his waist and put the rattles around his neck. With the fawn's skin over his shoulders and the pipe in his mouth, he looked more like an Indian than ever.

Champlain was kneeling on the sand beside the chief. As was his custom, he was drawing with a twig a rough map of the coast they had been passing. He always used whatever was at hand for his maps—mud, birch bark, paper if he had it—this time, sand. The chief recognized the wide bay where they were and the big harbor with many islands. Champlain put six pebbles at different places on the map. A few days before when he drew a map, another chief had done this.

Panonias had told him that they must stand for different tribes but as the language on this part of the coast was strange both to him and to his wife, he could not be sure. The chief nodded and grunted. This did not help much, but now he took the twig in his own hand and continued the map by drawing the outline of a cape. It was like a man's arm and elbow and clenched fist. He pointed to the ship, put a chip of wood to show where it lay, then moved it far out to sea.

"He means we must travel a long way out to sea before we try to double that cape," Champlain said.

They sailed the next day, leaving presents of kettles and knives and beads for their hosts. Etienne played the zither as they left and the last thing they saw was the dancing ring of Indians.

They had to head north to keep the wind from driving them on that white sandy shore, but at last they were traveling along the seaward side of the cape. One evening they anchored in a quiet green harbor. Tom, who went ashore with Panonias, reported that the Indians seemed friendly and that Nauset seemed to be their name for the harbor.

Champlain came ashore. There was another map-drawing on the beach and he learned of large islands far out to sea. Tom pointed to his master's white collar, then took sand in his hand, let it fall through his fingers, and shivered.

"How deep does this white stuff fall?" he asked, showing various depths with his hand. "So high? So high?"

The Indians showed him a depth of about a foot. By other signs he tried to find out if the harbor ever froze over. He thought they said that it did not but he could not be sure.

They might have tried to make their settlement there if it had not been for the kettle. It was an ordinary iron kettle, though larger than some. Five sailors had gone ashore, each taking a kettle to get fresh water. The Indians, so friendly half an hour before, snatched one of the kettles. The sailor struggled to keep it. He was wounded with arrows, then killed with knives. Muskets were fired from the ship. The Indians ran off in terror.

The other sailors now buried the body of the dead man. They took one of the Indians prisoner and brought him back to the ship. The Sieur de Monts asked if the prisoner was one of the murderers. The sailors admitted that he had not killed their comrade. De Monts, a just and merciful man, ordered them to release him. Other Indians appeared and made signs that they too were not guilty of the killing. The sailors on the ship would have fired their muskets into the crowd but de Monts would not allow them to punish the innocent as a lesson to the guilty. They started back for St. Croix.

"There are no furs," Tom heard de Monts say to his master, "and the shores are alive with savages who will dance for you one minute and kill you for a kettle the next. This is no place for our colony."

"You will spend another winter at St. Croix then?" Champlain asked.

De Monts shuddered and said no.

"You remember," he asked, "the harbor we found in Acadia that we named Port Royal? What would you think of settling there?"

Champlain thought well of it. The harbor was well protected from storms. On the north, hills would shut off the bitterest of the winter winds. There were springs of fresh water, streams, pleasant meadows, plenty of wood for building and for fires. The soil would be better there than at St. Croix, where vegetables had grown well at first but where, in summer, the gardens had dried up because the ground was too sandy.

They agreed to move. Luckily snow came late that year. Before it fell they were eating wild ducks in the hall of their new habitation at Port Royal. The doors and windows they had brought from France were moved from St. Croix to the new buildings. This habitation was smaller and more compact than the one at St. Croix. There was a house for de Monts in which some of the best woodwork was used. De Monts himself returned to France to see to the business of the fur trading company there. He left Captain Pontgravé behind as

Governor of Port Royal and of all North America, for France claimed it all.

Many of the survivors of St. Croix returned to France. Among those brave enough to face another winter were Champlain, his servant Thomas, Etienne Brulé and Nicholas Marsolet. New colonists had come with Pontgravé. There were about forty-five in all at Port Royal.

This does not count Minette, who had landed long before the habitation was finished and who was already striking terror into the hearts of rats and mice. With her were cats of various sizes and colors. It was becoming hard to tell whether they were her children or her grandchildren or not related to her at all. The huge black cat had gone back to France and a tigerish-looking gentleman with yellow eyes had taken his place. He lived chiefly at the mill where grain was ground by hand and where there was a good supply of rats.

Some of these were black rats of old Norman ancestry. Their ancestors had traveled back and forth across the Channel with William the Conqueror. Others were gray rats of less distinguished families but just as good appetite. The Old Man, as the younger rats called the guardian of the mill, found them all good eating. In his opinion a rat tasted best when it was about six months old and had been fattened on just the right amount of grain. The kittens took whatever they could get.

That winter was less severe than the last one but still there was scurvy and some men died. Grinding grain was a dreary task and the men took their turns at it sullenly. The houses had been built of green logs. They shrank and the icy cold found its way through the chinks. The bay froze. It was hard work to chop through the ice and bring up oysters with wooden tongs. Luckily hunting was good. The hunters brought in hares and partridges. The fishermen caught plenty of fish.

One day Tom, who was coming home with a pailful of smelts he had caught, found himself surrounded by a band of curious Indians who admired his blond hair and strange clothes. Their own clothes were cloaks of skins patched together, slung over one shoulder, leaving the other bare. They wore leggings and moccasins of deerskin. Their black hair was crowned with moose hair dyed red. Porcupine quills colored red, black and white were their necklaces.

The chief of this party was a tall genial Indian named Membertou. Most Indians considered the Frenchmen's beards hideous. They had little hair on their own faces and they pulled out any that grew. Membertou, however, was rather proud of a tuft of stringy black hair on his chin. He claimed to be more than a hundred years old. He remembered when Jacques Cartier sailed up the St. Lawrence more than sixty years before, he said. His tribe belonged to the Algonquin Indians. Before long Etienne and Tom found they could talk with him. The Indians learned French rapidly. Champlain noticed that though they had trouble in pronouncing V and F, they soon spoke French better than did those colonists who had been born in Gascony.

The Indians brought moose meat, seal oil and furs to trade. Several went off with French jackets of red cloth. Others got beads and knives and kettles. Membertou came back often to see them. He was the first Indian to become a Christian. He was, Tom thought, in his cheerfulness, patience and generos-

ity more truly a Christian than many of the sullen, grumbling Frenchmen.

Spring came early in 1606. Champlain had worked all winter making fair copies of his charts. Real seagoing charts they were, with soundings of treacherous reefs and safe entrances to harbors clearly marked. These difficult coasts with their many capes and peninsulas, their twisting rivers, hidden shoals and tremendous tides were somehow reduced to beautifully drawn and lettered maps.

Now that it was spring, Champlain was glad to lay down his pen and take up a spade. With Tom's help he dammed up a little brook and made a trout pool and another saltwater pool for sea fish. They made a garden with a summerhouse in it and planted flowers and vegetables. There were open meadows near the garden. Small birds liked the place too. They chirped and warbled and sang there.

That summer a new shipload of colonists arrived. De Monts stayed in France trying to organize the fur trading company. In his place came the Sieur de Poutrincourt, to whom all the land around Port Royal had been granted as his estate. Of the new colonists the most interesting to Tom was Marc Lescarbot, lawyer, poet and historian. There was always something going on where Lescarbot was. He wrote verses for every occasion. He encouraged dancing and singing in harmony. He planned plays and pageants and planted gardens.

Vegetables did well at Port Royal that year. Lescarbot said to Tom that with corn, wine, cattle, linen, wool and iron, Frenchmen could have a better treasure in Canada than all the gold in Mexico.

Of course, Tom thought, he hasn't seen the winter yet.

Some of those who had lived through a winter thought the colony ought to be moved farther south. Champlain still dreamed of his city on the rock with its shining towers. For the present, however, they decided to keep the Port Royal habitation. They broke up into three groups. One went back to France with Pontgravé. Lescarbot with old Membertou and a second group of colonists stayed at Port Royal, Poutrincourt and Champlain set off south along the coast.

The voyage was much like the one the year before. They used Champlain's charts and before long found themselves sailing along the ocean side of the cape with the white beaches and passing the green harbor where the sailor had been killed for a kettle the year before. They anchored in a harbor farther along the coast. They set up a cross with the arms of France carved on it and they talked of making their settlement there.

Nearby there was a good-sized Indian village with round wigwams. Bayberries, beach plums and wild roses grew along the shore. At first the Indians were friendly. Tom dressed a wound—a cut on the foot—for one of them. The Indian was delighted with the bandage. The next time Tom saw him he had it around his head for an ornament.

The only drawbacks seemed to be the mosquitoes and the innumerable fleas with which the Indians were covered.

Unfortunately, they found, these were not the only difficulties.

Suddenly Poutrincourt looked at the Indian village and said to Champlain, "They are taking down their wigwams—a bad sign, I think."

Some of the sailors had set up an oven on shore and were

baking bread. Poutrincourt ordered them back to the ship. Some came promptly but five stayed by the fire, eating hot bread. Indians, hiding among the trees, shot at the Frenchmen with arrows, killing some, wounding others. The terrible war whoops of killing Indians were heard for the first time. The sound of French muskets rang out in answer. The French went ashore and buried the bodies. They rescued Jean Duval, a locksmith, and brought him back to the ship.

As they sailed away they saw the savages tearing down the cross and digging up the bodies. They were yelping and howling like wolves and waving the dead men's shirts in the air.

The idea of settling south of Port Royal was given up.

On November 14th, 1606, Membertou's keen eyes saw the sails of Champlain's ship in the distance. For weeks Lescarbot and the men at Port Royal had been getting ready for this moment. The longboat was rowed fast down the harbor to meet the ship. The boat towed a dinghy painted blue. When they reached the ship, a strange figure, dressed in blue with a long beard of seaweed, stood up in the dinghy. He raised a trident in his right hand. His words of welcome traveled clearly across the water to the ship:

> *"Stop, Sagamores, and listen. Stop and stare!*
> *You see a god who has you in his care.*
> *Do you not know me? Saturn was my father*
> *And I am Neptune, Jupiter's own brother."*

"I believe that's Lescarbot behind that seaweed beard!" Tom said excitedly to his master.

Tom thought the play was the most wonderful thing he had ever seen. He liked the long string of verses, prophesying that a thousand French ships would ride those waters some day. It was wonderful, he thought, when the Tritons, who rowed the long boat, blew their trumpets and spoke in verse. One of the Tritons was Nicholas. Another, painted like an Indian, was Etienne.

When the Tritons came on board, the Sieur de Poutrincourt courteously drew his sword and raised it in salute. These Indian followers of Neptune brought gifts of moose meat, beaver skins and fish. Among them were an Indian Cupid and an Indian Diana who recited lines mixing up French and Indian words. At last everyone sang in harmony:

> *"Good Neptune gives us*
> *Against the waves assurance*
> *And says we'll surely*
> *All meet again in France."*

More trumpets sounded. Cannon roared. Even the cook who welcomed them to dinner spoke in verse. Lescarbot called this first North American pageant "The Theatre of Neptune." It was the happy beginning of a good winter. There was little snow, little sickness, plenty of fresh fish and game.

Champlain and Lescarbot established what they called the Good Time Order. A gold chain was given to the best hunter of the day to wear at dinner. This aroused rivalry and many kinds of game were brought in. Dinner was served formally with toasts and music. Each man at the high table, where Champlain and Poutrincourt sat, took his turn in being steward of the order. He would spend two days before the dinner in planning it with the cooks and in going out with the hunters to get some special delicacy for it. He would oversee the cooking himself, taste the sauces, season the soup.

When all was ready he would put on the collar of the order— it was worth four crowns—around his neck, take his staff of office in his hand and march into the dining hall. Behind him paraded the members of the order, each carrying a dish. When the first course had been cleared away, they would bring in the dessert with the same ceremony. After the meal was over, the steward would propose a toast to the steward of the next day and hand over his staff of office and the collar.

Hungry Indian squaws were fed from the kitchen but when Membertou and his sagamores came to visit, they were seated at the high table where they behaved with great dignity, listening gravely to the speeches, Lescarbot's verses, and to the music. Poutrincourt loved music. He composed it himself, some of it for Indian religious services. Often the sagamores gathered around Etienne while he played French dance tunes on his zither. They were handsome figures in their robes of soft white moose skin ornamented with designs in red and violet blue. Their faces were painted in the same colors.

Tom, who knew their language by this time, had heard them say what they thought of the looks of some of the French carpenters and masons and locksmiths. There was no doubt that, compared with certain hairy, squinting, round-shouldered, bowlegged fat Frenchmen, the tall Indians were fine-looking men. Their teeth were white, their eyes were keen, they could swim like salmon and run as fast as the Sieur de Poutrincourt's gray hounds.

Of course the Frenchmen had their own opinions about the Indians. They were dirty, they said. The Indians never washed their hands. They would hold a piece of meat in the mud while they tore it apart with their hands. Their children were spoiled. A papoose would cry and its mother, who was sewing a canoe with spruce roots, would have to get up from her work with the baby on her back and dance until the crying stopped. The men did not fight properly with their fists, breaking noses and flattening ears as Frenchmen did. They wrestled in the mud, pulling each other's hair and biting. Savages, that's what they were, and lazy! They would smoke and eat and tell stories and sleep all day.

Tom loved these storytellings. Sometimes a speaker would go on for two hours while his friends laughed at his jokes. They were great laughers and would listen to the same long stories of hunts and battles over and over again, laughing in the right places.

It was true that the squaws did most of the hard work. They cooked, made the bark dishes, carried wood for the fires, dressed skins for leggings and moccasins, calked the canoes with spruce gum, carried the heaviest loads and were beaten regularly to keep them from being idle. However, no one who went hunting with the Indian men and had seen them make a cabin or a palisade thought they were lazy.

The Indians despised the French for haggling over the price of furs.

"You are rich. We are poor. You should give generously," they would say.

The French never found a good answer to this statement.

One of the chiefs once asked Tom if he knew if the King of France had a son.

"Yes," Tom said. "His name is Prince Louis."

"I may let him marry my daughter," the chief said thoughtfully. "But he must give me a good present, nothing stingy. I must have four or five barrels of biscuit, plenty of beans, bows, harpoons and some tobacco and a fine red cloak."

The chief then asked what kind of house the King lived in.

"As high as that tree," Tom said pointing to an eighty-foot pine.

The chief grunted.

"Is your king so tall?" he asked.

"No taller than you," Tom said. "Shorter perhaps."

"Why does he need such a tall house? We carry our wigwams and go where we please. Can the King's squaw take down his house and carry it on her back?"

"The King is rich," Tom said. "He has other houses and can visit them when he pleases."

"If the French are so rich, why do they come to our poor country? They must be poor. They have no beaver."

The Indians not only thought the French stingy and poor, they also considered them lazy. The daughter of one of the chiefs wished to marry a young Indian who worked in the kitchen at Port Royal. He had given up hunting and fishing because he was interested in French cooking. He used the herbs from the Port Royal gardens in sauces and he learned to make a fish stew of lobsters, mussels and saffron with chunks of French bread in it rubbed with garlic butter that was very popular with the Good Time Order.

The chief forbade the marriage. He was sure that a man who was too lazy to go hunting would never provide properly for his daughter. However, the young bridegroom went fishing and brought back such a fine catch of salmon that the chief decided to allow the marriage after all. The bridegroom was permitted to go back to his kettles. The salmon with butter and duck-egg sauce he served that night was eaten with great enthusiasm.

The gardens grew well that spring of 1607. The colony seemed to be well established but de Monts' secretary arrived from France with bad news. De Monts was no longer head of the fur trading company. The colonists were ordered to return to France. In August, Champlain harvested his grain to show the King what crops could be grown in New France, made a roll of his charts—the best maps so far of North America—and sailed for France.

Just before the ship sailed he said to Tom, "I have not given up my plans. They are only postponed. Stay with Membertou. Learn to think and speak like an Indian. We will win an empire yet for France and bring Christianity to these poor savages. Some day someone—not I, not you perhaps—will find a way to the Pacific. Whether the Indians become our friends or our enemies depends much on our interpreters. I will do my part in France. Do yours here."

Just before the ship sailed, Membertou returned victorious and happy from a war against a tribe which had killed one of his kinsmen. Lescarbot wrote a poem about the victory, which

Tom translated to the sagamores. Tom felt that they did not exactly recognize their battles in Lescarbot's poetic version. Still, they listened with grave politeness. While Membertou made a fine long speech of friendship for the French, Lescarbot, never idle a minute, wrote one last poem —or perhaps he had it ready in his pocket. It was called "Farewell to New France" and it told about all the animals Lescarbot had seen—hummingbirds, eagles, muskrats, caribou. They had a caribou on the ship. They planned to give it to the King. It would have a happy life, Lescarbot said, in the Royal Gardens.

Tom wondered about that. Perhaps, he thought, the caribou was like most of the Indians who went to France. They could stand being half starved in the snowy wilderness but they could not bear being cooped up in a French palace. Without freedom they died.

CHAPTER 5

QUEBEC

THE HABITATION seemed gloomy and dull after Champlain and Lescarbot left. No Good Time Order now, no poems at breakfast, no plays in the Great Hall after dinner. The young Indian who had taken such an interest in cooking went back to hunting and fishing. His wife did the cooking in Indian style. She threw half-cleaned fish and stringy meat into a kettle made by hollowing out a piece of a log. Then she heated stones and threw them into the water until the meat was more or less cooked. Her father was delighted that her husband had turned out so well after all.

A few Frenchmen had been left to guard the habitation and Membertou had been invited to use it during the winter. However, by the time snow fell, the Indians took down their wigwams and wandered along frozen rivers and forest trails in search of deer and moose. Tom went with them. He dressed like an Indian now in leggings and moccasins of deerskin with a cloak of squirrel skins patched together over his shoulder. He had outgrown his French clothes, except for the blue camlet cloak with the red lining. This was a garment much admired by the Indians. Tom saved it for grand occasions such as a *tabagie* when they killed a moose.

With his blond hair and blue eyes, Tom made a rather odd-looking Indian. One of Membertou's favorite jokes was that he would like Tom's scalp to add to his collection. The sagamores always roared with laughter when Membertou said this. Of course Tom laughed too, out of politeness, but he never heard this joke without a prickly feeling around the top of his head.

His hair had grown down to his shoulders. He pleased the squaws by letting them cut it off with one of his surgical knives. The hair, which curled slightly, was much treasured. It was used, along with dyed moose hair, shell beads and porcupine quills, in decorating headbands. Making the shell beads was an endless task. Large cockleshells were fished up out of certain secret places in the sea. The squaws would break a shell into hundreds of pieces. These pieces they would smooth for hours on heated stones until they were rounded. Then they pierced them, just how Tom never knew. Perhaps this part of the work was a secret. He never saw them do it.

Some of the beads were white and some purple. The beads they got from the French were brighter and of more colors but the shell beads were more highly valued than the glass beads from across the sea. No French lady thought more of her pearls than the Indians did of their shell beads.

French hatchets were another matter. Every Indian wanted one. He stopped using a stone axe as soon as he could get a metal one. Champlain had left Tom a supply of hatchets and beads to trade for furs and his pack soon had many beaver skins in it.

He traded one of his hatchets for a pair of snowshoes and he learned to walk quickly and steadily on them. He walked like an Indian now, with his toes slightly turned in. The Indians laughed at the way the French turned out their toes. That was how a seal would look if he walked on snowshoes, Membertou said.

He imitated a seal walking on snowshoes and getting tripped because he crossed one end over the other. Then Membertou's sons and grandsons and great-grandsons all walked like seals on snowshoes and tripped and rolled in the snow, laughing till their ribs ached.

Tom enjoyed the Indians when they did not have their company manners on. He liked the things they taught him—how to keep from getting snow blindness by making himself wooden goggles with slits in them, how to tell the tracks of different animals in the snow, how to catch the beaver in his house. Tom liked the clear winter nights when the stars blazed in the sky and then suddenly vanished in clouds of white and green northern lights.

He learned to sleep comfortably on the ground. Fifteen men could sleep in a wigwam with their feet towards the central fire and be warm all night. Tom remembered how Lescarbot had said that the French could live well if they had wool, linen, cattle, corn, wine and iron—that these were the real riches. Membertou's tribe had none of these things but they lived and enjoyed life. There was little illness among them but sometimes Tom had a chance to practice what he had learned from the surgeon at St. Croix.

Once the tribe was trailing a bull moose. The snow was not very deep and though they had followed him for two days, he showed no signs of tiring. Tom and one of Membertou's grandsons were ahead of one of the other hunters. They were crossing a snow-covered pond. The moose was near a little hill at the other end of it.

He turned and saw them. For a moment he stood still, his horns like great jagged fans against the snow-covered hill. Tom did not see him start to move. He only heard the thunder of his hoofs as he plunged head down across the pond. Tom shot an arrow, another, a third at the charging moose. Two of them struck him. They made no more impression than a mosquito bite, only angered him more perhaps. The young Indian bravely ran towards the moose with his spear. In a moment the boy was a heap in the snow. Blood gushed from a deep wound in his arm, staining the snow where he lay.

Tom ran towards him. He heard the shouts of the hunters from the woods, heard arrows singing past him, saw the moose wheel and charge up the hill again. The young Indian had a broken leg as well as a wounded arm. Tom stopped the bleeding with a tourniquet, sewed up the wound and, with the help of Membertou, who was the medicine man of the tribe, set the leg and put it in splints.

With the Indians a broken leg often meant lameness for life. Tom had seen more than one Indian limping, one leg an inch shorter than the other, because his leg had been broken and never set.

In their wanderings they had swung around in the direction of Port Royal. The injured Indian was loaded on a toboggan and dragged by the squaws across snow and frozen rivers and the still-icy harbor to the habitation. There were crutches there, left by the surgeon, and they fitted well enough. Tom was pleased to see his patient hopping briskly around on them. His arm healed cleanly though the marks of the seven stitches Tom had put into it would always show. Luckily all the Indians considered them a decoration.

Minette had spent an industrious winter. She and her descendants—there were all colors now, black, gray, white, striped tigers, even one yellow kitten with white paws—had kept the habitation free of rats and mice. They had also, when the weather turned warm and the ice melted on Champlain's trout pond, helped themselves to a good many trout. Minette brought up all the kittens. She did not trust their mothers to teach them how to wash their faces properly. The mothers, she felt, were quite careless enough to allow their children to rub their ears before they licked their paws instead of after as a well-educated kitten should. Only a great-grandmother knows just how to help a kitten when its purr gets stuck, Minette thought. And as for teaching them how to watch a mouse hole properly!

Young people have no patience these days, Minette said to herself, cuffing a young tiger kitten who should have been on duty at the second mouse hole to the left of the kitchen door and not chasing her tail in front of the fire.

She received Tom politely but he was not sure if she really remembered him. He found her bag hanging up by his bed and held it out to her. Minette at once tried to get into it. It was a tight squeeze but she managed it. Her descendants were much surprised to see their great-grandmother riding like a papoose on Tom's back and looking over his shoulder.

The Indians stayed at Port Royal till the ice went out.

"Now we will go to Tadoussac and meet our good friend there," Membertou said one April morning. "He will come soon."

It was extraordinary, Tom thought, how news traveled in this vast empty country. Like most news, before or since, it was not always true, but it was at least something to talk about when the tobacco pipes had been smoked.

He knew that the Basque fishermen who came to the Grand Banks for codfish often came on shore to get fresh meat and sometimes a few furs. They heard rumors on French wharves and passed them on to the Indians in *baragouin*. They went from one tribe to another in various Indian dialects. This time the news was brought by one of Membertou's grandsons.

He said that the Sieur de Monts was head of the fur trading again, that Pontgravé was now on the way, bringing Champlain. The French, he said, were going to build a new habitation at Tadoussac. The doors and windows for it were on the ship.

Some of this news must be true, Tom thought, but before he could know, there was a long journey by canoe and many portages ahead of him. They arrived at Tadoussac in time to see Pontgravé's ship come up the river. There he was on deck, fatter and redder in the face than ever, shouting so loud that there was an echo of "Malouins" from the dark cliffs.

"No," he called, "Champlain is not with me. His ship will come soon."

He waved his hand. Membertou's sharp eyes saw sails down

the river. The Indians all jumped into their canoes and started paddling out into the St. Lawrence. The wind was with the ship. The tide was with the canoes. There was choppy blue water and green foaming whirlpools ahead but the canoes slipped rapidly downstream and were soon circling the ship.

Champlain heard the shouts of the paddlers and came on deck. He marveled, as he always did, at the speed and grace with which the Indians drove their canoes through rough water. People in France smiled in polite disbelief when he told them that a canoe could carry three men and their food, weapons and a load of valuable furs and that a boy could carry the canoe on his head as easily as a Frenchman could wear his beaver hat.

Champlain had felt strange in France. The dark streets of Paris had seemed colder on rainy winter days than Port Royal in a snowstorm. He had forgotten how filthy the streets were and how hard it was to get a cup of pure water to drink. He missed his trout stream and his gardens. Even the grandest dinners did not taste so good as that fish stew he had carried in one night for the Good Time Order.

He had been away three years from France but the gentlemen who swept off their beavers, wide-brimmed and glossy with the newest ornaments of feathers, ribbons and flowers, had not missed him. They had no idea of the toil and danger it took to bring a beaver skin from deep in the Canadian wilderness to a French hatter's shop. They were very particular about the height of the crown and just how the brim on the right side must be looped up so it would not be in the way of their swords in case there was a duel to fight. It did not interest them to hear that to catch a beaver you must find both doors to his house and frighten him away from the back entrance. Nor did they care to hear about how you must reach into the front door under icy water, ready to seize him by the neck before he tore your hand with his fierce sharp teeth.

His friends, Champlain thought, were in Canada and now here they were all around him, sweeping past the ship like a school of porpoises. They made circles and figure eights. They stood up in the canoes yelling with their hands clapped against their mouths. They splashed water with their paddles. Under the freshly painted red and violet stripes he began to recognize faces he knew. There was Membertou with his tuft of black beard. He was paddled by two painted braves with eagle feathers in their hair. The one in the bow had something strange about him—a white head looking over his shoulder and yellow hair.

"Thomas!" Champlain called. "Thomas!" and Tom held up his shining paddle in salute.

The ship with its escort of canoes soon reached Tadoussac but the Basque fishermen had been wrong. The new settlement was not to be there.

"Better than that," Champlain explained to Tom. "At last I have persuaded the King and the Sieur de Monts that our colony must be where the Indians can easily bring their furs. Our habitation will be in a place easy to defend. Can you guess where?"

"Quebec?" asked Tom, his eyes flashing with excitement.

"Yes," his master said, "in the shadow of the rock."

He added that for the trading they could go farther up the river, if necessary as far as the place Cartier had known as

Hochelaga. He had named a high mountain there Mount Royal and Frenchmen were beginning to call it Montreal.

"There is a great fall of water there," Champlain said. "It travels for miles as fast as an eagle flies, boiling in whirlpools, sliding over rocks, foaming past islands. It is as if a whole ocean of water were trying to get free. And some think," he said in a lower tone, "that it leads to another ocean, to the Pacific, that it leads to China, so they call the fall La Chine Rapids."

"That would be a good trading place," Tom said. "I remember on your charts, sir, how the river of the Iroquois flows into the St. Lawrence farther down. The Indians who bring the furs will be safe from the Iroquois if we meet upstream at the rapids. I have heard much talk of that since I have been at Tadoussac."

"You understand the Indian speech then?" Champlain asked.

"Better than I did at first but I have much to learn," Tom answered. "Each tribe speaks a little differently from the others but I can understand the Algonquins and the Montagnais fairly well. Our friends tell me that they cannot understand the Iroquois or the Hurons at all. Those two tribes, they say, speak nearly the same tongue, though they are great enemies. All the tribes I have met so far belong to the Algonquin race, Membertou says. It seems it is no easier for a Huron to understand an Algonquin than it is for an Englishman to talk French."

"Or for me to speak anything but the French of Brouage," Champlain said smiling. "Yet every now and then some rare bird can chatter in both."

Tom said that people who spoke both English and French were not uncommon. There was a family at Dieppe, the Kirkes, whose mother was French and whose father was English. Like the Lees, they traded back and forth across the channel. They spoke either language well.

"There were five of them, fine-looking tall young men, a little older than I. If you saw them on an English wharf they were as stiff-backed and frozen-faced as any Englishman. Then you'd meet them at Dieppe and they'd talk with their elbows and their shoulders and their eyebrows, smiling like good Frenchmen. We should have some of them here—they'd learn Huron for you, sir!"

Champlain said kindly, "I am satisfied with my own interpreters. Pontgravé tells me that Etienne and Nicholas have done well too."

"They speak well and they have brought in good packs of furs," Tom said.

It was early in June when Champlain had reached Tadoussac. He set his carpenters to work at once, fitting out a pinnace to take them to Quebec. They sailed her up the river on June 30th. Before long they saw the white rush of Montmorency Falls and the big island where wild grapevines twined themselves into the trees. On July 3rd, 1608, Tom saw for the first time the great rock of Quebec, dark against a blue and white sky. He and Minette and two of her grandchildren, both white, were in the first boatload of settlers to set foot on the narrow strip of land below the rock. Within a few moments Minette had caught her first rat, also a passenger on the pinnace, and Tom was helping to unload materials for building the first permanent settlement north of Florida in North America.

As usual, doors and window frames and other woodwork had been brought from France. The pinnace went back and

forth to Tadoussac bringing loads from the ships there while foundations and walls were rising at Quebec. Champlain had drawn a plan for the new habitation. It showed three buildings close together, each thirty feet long and nineteen wide. They were two stories high, with steeply pitched roofs. There was also a warehouse. There were tall dovecotes. A gallery for defense ran around the buildings. There was a moat with a drawbridge. Cannon on raised platforms pointed towards the river and there was a strong palisade. Sheltered by the massive rock behind, it would be, Champlain said proudly, a strong fortress.

Before snow fell it was complete with a shining sun dial high on the front of the main building and the blue and white flag with the lilies of France waving above it. Outside the palisades, gardens had been laid out. On Champlain's plan they looked like small flowered rugs. There would be flowers in them someday, Tom felt sure.

Before the habitation was finished, they lived in huts along the river. Among the men who worked on the habitation was Jean Duval, the locksmith who had been rescued from the savages in the fight on one of the beaches of what Champlain called the White Cape. There were several locksmiths among the colonists. Antoine Natel, a timid-looking round-shouldered little man, was another. Tom wondered why the colony needed so many locksmiths. Was it perhaps because, in France, they had picked locks for thieves as often as they had made them for honest men? There were many petty criminals among the settlers although there were honest hardworking men too. Many of the criminals had done nothing worse than steal a loaf of bread or set a trap for a rabbit, but in France you could be thrown into prison for snaring a rabbit in your own field.

It was Champlain's habit to judge men by how they worked in Canada, not by how they had lived in France. He was too busy having ditches and cellars dug to notice that Jean Duval, after the day's work was over, always walked with one man alone and a different one each time. Duval never chose Tom for one of these private talks and, like his master, Tom suspected nothing.

Then, one day, the pinnace came up the river from Tadoussac. Champlain sent Tom on an errand to her Captain, a man called Testa. Tom had given his message and was about to leave when Antoine Natel's stooping figure appeared in the cabin doorway.

He stood there a moment, twisting his blackened hands together, his face gray and shining with sweat. Then, in a voice they could hardly hear, with the words tumbling over each other, he managed to stammer out his story.

There was a plot, he said, trembling as he spoke. It would be any night now, as soon as the pinnace went down to Tadoussac and Pontgravé to France. Then the Basque fur traders would sail up the river. The Basques hated de Monts and the fur company because they had spoiled the Basques' fur trade. Captain Testa knew that, didn't he? Captain Testa of course knew it. There had been several clashes with the Basques. Pontgravé had been wounded in a fight with a Basque ship and Champlain had had to make peace between them.

"Now," said Natel, his voice steadying a little, "Jean Duval has plotted with the Basques against the Sieur de Champlain.

He talked separately with each workman. With the others he did as with me, promising me a knife in my back some night if I refused to join. That's how he begins the talk, staring you in the eyes with a big knife pointing at you, asking if you'd like to try the edge, asking how you'd like to feel the point in your back or in your heart."

Most of the workmen, Natal went on to say, would not have joined if they had not been frightened. There were only four really bad ones besides Duval.

"We all go trembling to bed at night," he added, "believe me, sir."

"Very well," Captain Testa said. "I believe you. The plan is—what?"

"Some night Duval will raise a false alarm. The Sieur de Champlain will be killed as he comes from his hut. If you resist," he turned to Tom, "you will be killed too. The fortress will then be Duval's. He'll sell it to the Basques, who will take care of you, Captain, at Tadoussac. Then, Duval says, we'll all be rich and go back to France. The Basques have promised him free passage."

Captain Testa said, "It's the plan of a pack of fools but it's dangerous nevertheless. What was it you told them you came for, Natel? Nails? Very well. Take a keg and go back to your work. It will be better for you to know nothing of what I plan. Go quickly. They may notice you have been gone too long."

When Natel had gone, Captain Testa said to Tom, "Your master asked me when I would be ready to start down to Tadoussac. Tell him that I have some sails to patch and other small repairs to make. I would like to get off tomorrow with the afternoon tide, but I might have to wait until the next day. Tell him where Duval can hear you if possible. Or at least in someone's hearing. It will get back to him. Then when you are alone with him in his hut, give him this note. Say nothing. You will almost certainly be spied on."

He sat writing for a few minutes and then gave Tom the folded paper.

"See that clump of woods over there. No, not that one, nearer the river with the clump of white birches. Can you guide your master to it? In the dark? I will be waiting there an hour after sunset."

"I understand, sir," Tom said.

He liked this brown-faced, brown-eyed, quick-speaking man. He reminded him a little of his master. This was the highest compliment Tom could pay anyone.

The great hall of the new habitation smelled of pine shavings and of good pea soup with ham in it. This was the first of the buildings to be used. It was still not quite finished. Champlain was sitting alone at the high table. The table was a pine board a yard wide, resting on trestles. Champlain was eating soup out of a pewter porringer and reading about Magellan's voyage to the Philippines. Jean Duval was putting a lock on the door of the pewter cupboard.

Tom crossed the hall with his light quick step, bowed to his master and gave him Captain Testa's message that the pinnace would not sail till the next day or the day after. Duval was twisting the key in the new lock as Tom passed him on his way to get his soup. He usually scowled at Tom but now he smiled almost pleasantly.

He's glad about the news, Tom thought.

He carried his soup to the table where he usually sat with Nicholas and Etienne when they were there. They had gone hunting deer with a band of Montagnais Indians so he was alone at the table. The workmen were beginning to leave their work. Four locksmiths were at a table together. Duval left the pewter cupboard and brought his bowl of soup to the locksmiths' table. They had wooden bowls and spoons but Duval was using a pewter bowl and a pewter spoon. Tom had made it himself, running the pewter into the spoon mold. The spoon had a French shield with the lilies of France on the handle. The spoons were so soft that they broke often. When there were enough broken Tom would melt them up and make some more.

Duval broke his spoon today and threw the pieces into his bowl. They fell with a dull clink. Antoine Natel looked up. He was stooped over his bowl, eating his food like a stray dog who knows a mastiff is watching him. There was a long loaf of freshly baked bread on the table. Duval could have broken off a piece as others did but he pulled out his knife, stabbed it into the bread, then cut off a chunk. More than one pair of eyes followed the flash of the knife as Duval moved it, cutting bread, reaching across the table for a knife full of butter, spearing pieces of meat, pointing it towards the high table where Champlain sat, turning the pages of his book and letting his soup get cold.

Tom thought the meal would never be over but it was at last. The carpenters went back to work on the sleeping quarters, the masons to stoning up walls for the moat, the locksmiths to the forge. Champlain was with a party who were digging a channel that would connect a little stream with the moat. Tom went with some of the Montagnais who were eel-fishing. These Indians never planted grain or pumpkins or saved anything for the winter except eels, which they preserved by hanging them in the smoke of their fires. The season for catching the eels was in September and October. It was now in full swing.

Tom almost forgot the locksmiths' plot that hot, blue and gold September afternoon. He had seen the leaves turn before at St. Croix and Port Royal but they had never looked so beautiful to him as they did along the St. Lawrence. The orange and scarlet of sugar maples shone brilliantly against dark forests of fir and hemlock. The birches Captain Testa had shown him were beginning to turn to gold. Across the river, maples were deep crimson, almost purple. There was purple too on the mountains north of the St. Lawrence and the river itself was a deep rippling blue.

The catch of eels was good. The squaws had the fires going and the fish were soon hanging in the smoke. It was almost dark when Tom left the wigwams and walked towards his master's hut, not hurrying. He must do nothing to call Duval's attention to him, so he moved no faster than usual.

Champlain was reading by the light of a candle, burning in a lantern of iron and glass, some of Duval's craftsmanship.

Tom laid Captain Testa's letter on the book and said in a low tone, "Read this, master. Say nothing."

Champlain read it in silence, then handed it to Tom.

The Captain had written only: "It is important that I see you alone an hour after sunset. Say nothing. Thomas will guide you. Testa."

Champlain said only, "It is time."

Tom handed him his cloak, his sword and his beaver hat. Champlain blew out the candle. They could hear crickets chirping fast in the warm darkness. Etienne must have come back, for from the great hall came the plinking of his zither and dancing feet.

"They are all there, I think," Champlain said.

Tom circled the hut before they started but found no one.

There was no moon yet but the sky was clear and full of stars. They followed a path to a beach on a small stream that ran into the river. Tom kept his canoe, his most precious possession, near the hut. He had traded many hatchets for it. He carried it to the beach on his head. His master carried the paddles. They went upstream for a while, landed on the opposite shore, portaged along a path through the spruces, then through rushes to a larger river. Tom had to paddle hard upstream to cross it. The swift current almost carried them past the landing place but they reached it—a sandy beach where a boat from the pinnace was already lying. They pulled the canoe up on the sand and were soon in the birch grove.

Testa and the mate of the pinnace were there. Champlain listened calmly to the story of the plot. Tom noticed that Captain Testa called Champlain "Your Excellency, the Governor." Actually, as Tom learned later, his master was now Lieutenant Governor of Canada though he had never mentioned it. He thanked Captain Testa, sweeping off his hat with grave politeness. The moon was just coming up and the hat was dark against it for a moment.

Tom had sometimes wondered why men loaded their heads with these heavy things.

Why, he thought suddenly. Of course, it's so they can take them off.

Champlain, having praised Testa for what he had done, was now suggesting a plan for dealing with the plotters. The Captain agreed to it and they parted.

Testa did not sail the next day. His sails, torn in a recent gale, were still being patched on the deck. He had told two loyal sailors of the plot. They invited Duval and the other ringleaders on board that evening for supper and a jug of wine.

Tom and his master made another canoe trip that night, this time to where the pinnace swung at her moorings in the dark river. It was very quiet. Tom's paddle sounded loud in the water but he knew that in the singing and shouting from the pinnace it would not be heard. The singers were below in the sailors' quarters. Captain Testa, the mate and other members of the crew were waiting on deck. It was easy to overpower the plotters. Only Duval resisted. He drew his knife but Champlain already had his arm in a grip that made him scream with pain and drop it, cursing.

Testa's crew bound the men and took them to the habitation. Champlain roused the whole colony and called them into the great hall.

The picture of that meeting stayed long in Tom's mind. He would see his master standing on the dais by the high table with his hat thrown down beside him, his hand on his sword. Light from lanterns Duval had made flickered dimly in the big room. In this half-darkness Duval with his little gray eyes, his angry gray face and blackened hands looked like a cornered rat. Etienne and Nicholas lounged against the wall. Minette had leaped on Tom's shoulder. The kittens were chasing their tails. From the forge came the sound of the smith's hammer. He was making fetters, Tom knew.

Champlain spoke briefly and clearly. He knew about the plot, he said. He knew that some of the men had been forced into it. He promised mercy to all who confessed. The men were glad enough to do so. They had been living in terror of Duval long enough, had dreamed too often of feeling his knife in their backs. The smith came in with handcuffs clanking. More than one man breathed more freely when he saw that there were only four pairs. Champlain, as lieutenant for the King and for the Sieur de Monts in Canada, had power to hang the plotters at once but he would not hang a man without a trial. He sent to Tadoussac for Pontgravé and his officers—luckily they had not left for France—and asked them to come to Quebec and act as judges.

The trial was held in the great hall. The conspirators were found guilty. Duval was condemned to death and hanged. The other four men were sent back in irons to France on Pontgravé's ship.

After the trial was over, Tom admired his master more than ever. On Testa's ship he had shown how quickly he could act when action was needed. Yet not once, either in the birch wood, on the ship or at the trial, had he spoken a word of anger. He had been patient and merciful. He had sought justice, not vengeance.

Justice having been done, the colony went back to work.

Antoine Natel went on making locks and hinges. Carpenters whistled more cheerfully than they had for weeks as they sawed and hammered. Tom melted up the broken spoons, including the one Duval had used, added more lead and antimony and ran the metal into the spoon mold. Before the first heavy snows fell in November, the habitation was ready to face the winter. Water was running into the moat and freezing. Rye and wheat had sprouted in the gardens. Wood for fires in the great hall was stacked outside. The storehouse was full of food.

The Montagnais lived on their smoked eels till January. They caught a few beavers and brought the skins back to Quebec. With them were Nicholas and Etienne. They had learned to live happily in the smoke and dirt of the wigwams. They could travel for miles on snowshoes, following the trail of a moose.

Tom, whose duties that winter were keeping accounts, carrying firewood and acting as interpreter for Indians who came to the habitation, wished he too could be out on the hunting trails. Of course the stories were a good deal alike. "Well, this moose," Etienne would begin, "was the biggest moose I've ever seen—bigger than the biggest horse in France, wasn't he, Nicholas?"

"Much bigger—and what horns!" Nicholas would say.

"And swift!" Here Etienne would whistle. "He plunged through the snow at first like water down the rapids. That snow was just flying out from under his feet. Right, Nicholas?"

"Right! He went so fast we lost him. But we didn't give up, did we, Etienne?"

"Give up! I rather think not! How long was it we followed his trail before we saw him again? A day?"

"More than that. We slept in that cave, don't you remember?" Nicholas would answer.

This would go on about as long as the moose hunt, Tom sometimes thought, until at last the unlucky moose fell from weariness in the deep snow and—this was always part of the story—wept before he died.

Once Tom tried to tell his story about the moose that charged Membertou's grandson but Etienne and Nicholas were not interested. Tom had to listen while they told how the squaws came and skinned and cut up the moose. They put chunks of it in their log kettles with snow and hot stones. After a few hours of this the moose would be somewhat cooked.

"And then I suppose you ate the stones," Tom said. "They are usually the best part."

Etienne laughed but Nicholas drew his black brows together and said, "How witty people get who sit by the fire all winter!"

They went off again before long but other bands of Montagnais came from time to time. Their eels were used up and they were starving. Champlain gave them bread and beans. One band was so hungry that they ate the carcass of a dead dog they found in the snow. Some went back to their hunting but some stayed and lived on French provisions. Those who did got scurvy, which was beginning to break out among the French.

"It's because they eat our salt provisions," Champlain said to Tom.

The Indians never used salt themselves. It was true that they did not have scurvy so long as they had fresh meat or fish. However, both were scarce that winter and it was not unusual for Tom to find an Indian sick with scurvy, lying in the snow, never making a sound of complaint, while inside the habitation the Frenchmen groaned around the fire.

Tom did what he could for them but it was never enough. One day when an especially bitter wind streamed out of the north, Tom saw a group of Indians on the other side of the St. Lawrence starting to cross on the ice. At the time it looked solidly frozen, but the rapid current from upstream meeting the rising tide made the crossing treacherous. The Indians were halfway across when a great crack appeared ahead of them. They tried to jump it but it widened rapidly. Another came behind them. The ice all around them broke into big slabs. Some of the unfortunate people—they were mostly women and children and old men—vanished into the cold green water.

One little group seemed safe on a cake of ice big and strong enough to hold them, traveling straight towards the Quebec shore. Suddenly it spun around and was whirled out into the stream where the water was open and moving so fast that Tom knew the tide must have turned.

He could only watch horrified as the ice cake with the wailing, sobbing women holding out their hands to him spun swiftly towards the open water. Then came a grinding crash. Another huge cake of ice had crashed against the first one. It struck so hard that the Indians were thrown down on the ice. While they lay there, the force of the blow carried it close to the shore ice.

Before another crash could sink or break the floating cake Tom was on it, helping the Indians ashore, carrying small children, lifting a lame old man on his back. Most of the women got to their feet and leaped across the widening strip of water between the cake and the shore ice. It was on its way downstream again when Tom saw that what he had thought was only a heap of snow on the ice was moving slightly. Above the sound of wind and crashing ice, he heard something crying.

LAKE OF THE IROQUOIS

Tom jumped back to the ice cake.

The young woman lying there was dressed in white doeskins. She lay face down with her papoose on her back. The papoose was howling.

For his mother to get up and dance, Tom thought.

They were traveling fast downstream now but he saw that with luck they might strike on a small point of land. It thrust out from the shore just above where the river he had crossed, the night he and Champlain had met Captain Testa in the birch wood, flowed into the St. Lawrence. He knew that after its force struck the ice cake there would not be much hope for them. The cake was getting smaller and smaller and would soon tip them into the water. He put his hand on the woman's shoulder and spoke to her in Montagnais. She stirred but did not speak. She was unconscious. It was just as well perhaps.

They were close to the point now. Another piece of the cake split off. It tipped dizzily beneath his feet as it spun through the water.

Too small, Tom said to himself. Jump before it breaks.

He picked up the woman, howling papoose and all. She was taller than he but light and thin.

Starved, he thought, and heard a crack just under his feet.

He jumped. Water was around his knees, his waist, his shoulders, but there were rocks under his feet. He slipped and staggered out of the water, dragging rather than carrying the woman with him, and stumbled to the beach. As he laid the woman down in the snow and stood panting, he remembered that his snowshoes were still on the ice cake. He had taken them off before he made his jump to shore. The cake was edging away into the stream again.

He dashed back into the water and snatched his snowshoes off the ice cake. When he reached shore again there was not enough of it left to tell it from the rest of the jumbled, hurrying ice. He felt his leggings begin to stiffen.

This won't do. She'll freeze to death, he thought.

She was too heavy to carry any great distance. If he left her here and went for help, she might die in the snow. The Indians he had helped ashore had all hurried to the habitation. They were out of sight by now. He must do what he could. Perhaps, he thought, she would come out of her faint and be able to walk. He untied the papoose board from her back. The crying stopped and the small boy on it—he was too big really to be carried—stood up and stared at Tom.

Perhaps it was because he stopped crying that his mother at last opened her eyes. Tom noticed that they were chestnut rather than black eyes like most Indian eyes. Her hair too was not really black but had reddish brown lights in it.

"Can you walk if I help you?" he asked in Montagnais, but she did not speak. He must not have said it right.

She sat up and he held out his hands to help her get to her feet but he saw that something was wrong. She put her hands on her left leg and said something in words he did not understand. Her face changed from coppery to grayish olive green. He had seen Indians turn that color when they were in great pain. Like the others she made no sound, only looked up at him. A wounded deer had once given him the same look.

He knelt in the snow beside her and felt her leg. Yes, it was broken. He could feel that one end of the shinbone had slipped past the other. If he tried to move her, it might break through the skin. The papoose began to cry again. He was afraid to leave him near his mother so he carried him with him and set the board against a tree while he cut branches for splints from birch saplings. The papoose stopped crying at the sound of chopping.

He watched with interest while Tom cut strips from his own shirt to bind the splints in place and he was still quiet when Tom tipped the board up against a rock near where the woman was lying.

Tom knelt down beside her and explained to her what he was going to do. Afterwards he remembered that he had spoken to her not in her own tongue, which he did not know, nor in Montagnais, nor even in French but in English.

He said slowly: "Your leg is broken. I think I can fix it but I must hurt you. You must keep quite still. You will be brave, I know."

In some way the meaning of the words must have come to

her. She smiled up at him trustingly. She made no sound until Tom brought the ends of the bone together and had put on the splint. Then she spoke in her own language.

She's thanking me, Tom thought. But what shall I do with her now?

The answer came in a voice singing and the sound of a loaded toboggan sliding over crusty snow. It was Etienne coming back from hunting. He had his pack and the carcass of a deer on the toboggan. He cheerfully dumped the deer into the snow, helped Tom lift the woman onto the toboggan, put the papoose on Tom's back, then slung the deer over his shoulder. He went on singing as he swaggered off towards the habitation.

"Don't be late for supper, gosling. I think your passengers are hungry. Not that we needed any more mouths to feed just now. It would have been more sensible to leave them on the river," he called back.

He didn't, Tom knew, really mean it. There was something goodhearted about Etienne in spite of his rough speech and teasing ways. The Indians liked him and he had learned a good deal about them.

When they were moving the woman to the toboggan, Tom had said that she did not seem to understand Montagnais. Etienne had glanced quickly at her and at the papoose and had said, "Huron, perhaps. Her dress and the papoose board look like Huron work. Or perhaps Iroquois. I've been hunting with some Hurons and they tell me the Iroquois are their brothers, only they have quarreled. Well, there's nothing like a family fight, I always say."

Then he had gone off singing, leaving Tom to follow with the toboggan.

Etienne's guess was right. The woman was an Iroquois, as Tom found out from the Montagnais. She was a prisoner, captured with a band of Iroquois in a fight the summer before. The Montagnais gladly gave her and the little boy into Champlain's keeping. They said that she was too stupid to learn their tongue and she had been of little help in the eel-fishing. Now that she could only hobble on the crutches that Tom had made for her, she would be no use at all. Besides, Small Arrow, as she called her son, was too big for the papoose board. He was almost three. He should be standing on his own feet and learning to be a man.

Champlain had fed the Montagnais to keep them from starving though his own provisions were getting low. It was a relief when a message came from the men of the tribe that they had killed a moose ten miles away and that the women must come. That was all they saw of that particular band that winter.

The Iroquois woman recovered quickly but she limped a little and—Tom feared—always would.

"I'm afraid I'm not a very good surgeon," he said to Champlain, who replied, "Well, if I break my leg, you can set it."

Tom felt better.

He had learned to talk to his patient a little but he found the Iroquois tongue more difficult than the Algonquin dialects he had learned. The sounds seemed to come from the throat, never from the lips. He learned that the same phrase differently accented might mean something quite different. For instance a long string of sounds might mean "You have no sense" and with a slightly different accent "You are a liar." It was easy to see that strangers might get into trouble with speakers of such tongues.

However, by spring he was beginning to speak fairly well—or so Moon Rises told him. That was her name. Now that she was no longer starving she was a handsome woman. Small Arrow's legs had become strong now that he had enough to eat and they took him into all kinds of mischief. Tom was always rescuing him from the edge of the river or pulling him out of the fire with his hair singed, or keeping him out of the cook's kettles. Small Arrow had a mouthful of sharp white teeth with which he chewed everything that came his way. Leather straps, beans, salt pork, spruce gum, raw fish, old moccasins—everything seemed to agree with him.

One of his favorite sports was to run along with Rudolph, Champlain's big mastiff, holding him by an ear, a tail, anything that came in handy. Naturally if Small Arrow fell down, Rudolph's ear or tail would be yanked but the big dog only looked sadly at his companion. Once Tom saw Small Arrow kick Rudolph in the ribs. There was a low growl. Rudolph took the foot that had done the kicking and gently pressed his teeth into it, not enough to break the skin but so that the tooth prints showed clearly. Small Arrow never made a sound—and he never kicked Rudolph again.

What he loved most were Minette's two white grandchildren. They had grown long-legged during the winter. They liked to fight each other with soft paws, then fall down and suddenly begin chasing their own or each other's tails. They would drag fish heads all over the great hall, then run up to the top of the pewter cabinet and mew to be brought down. Tom taught Small Arrow to call the boy Miner and the girl Little Minette.

Small Arrow was never so happy as when he could catch both kittens and squeeze them against his face. This sign of affection resulted in his usually having a few scratches on his plump coppery cheeks. He talked to them in a *baragouin* of his own, part French, part Iroquois and part kitten talk. When they learned to purr, he learned too.

Moon Rises would smile when she heard him but her expression was usually a sad one. She would often stand for a long time looking up the river. She hoped her own people would come for her, she told Tom. Her husband had been killed by the Montagnais but she had another son, much older than Small Arrow, old enough to avenge his father's death, and a brother and an uncle, both chiefs of their tribe. If they knew where she was, they would come.

It was not, Tom knew, at all likely that they would come. He had been with Etienne and Nicholas up the St. Lawrence as far as the great fall, called La Chine Rapids by Champlain. He had seen where the river of the Iroquois joined the St. Lawrence. It was true that a war party could travel down that river and even attack Quebec, but to do so they would have to pass French ships and meet Huron, Algonquin and Montagnais canoes. Even if they knew Moon Rises and Small Arrow were at Quebec they were not likely to take such a risk for their sake.

What the Iroquois wanted was furs, French goods and their enemies' scalps. Their way of getting all three was to hide near a canoe portage and attack their enemies as they passed by with their loads. The Iroquois had been so successful in stealing and killing along the upper St. Lawrence that the Hurons no longer used it as a trade route. They either followed the Ottawa River, which met the St. Lawrence above Montreal, shooting the rapids to meet the French ships, or they went by a route through small rivers, lakes and wild forests that landed them at Three Rivers, between Quebec and Montreal. There was also a third route which, after endless portages, brought them out at Tadoussac.

Although Champlain always preferred peace to war, he had promised to help the Algonquins and Hurons against their enemies.

"It seems the only way to be sure of furs reaching the trading company," he said to Tom, "yet it would be best for them and for us if we could make peace between all these tribes."

"Let me do what I asked you, master," Tom said. "Peace might come that way."

What Tom had asked was permission to take Moon Rises and Small Arrow back to their own people. At this time of the year, Moon Rises said, her tribe would be camped on the lake out of which the River of the Iroquois flowed. She added that they would give many beaver and a fine belt of wampum if Small Arrow were brought back to his great-uncle. If her older son and her brother had been killed by the Montagnais—they had disappeared before she was captured—Small Arrow would be chief of the tribe some day. If he went back to his people, he would have many canoes and he would always be a friend of the Men of Iron.

That was what the Indians called the French because of their armor.

"There is a Montagnais who would go with us for a kettle and two axes," Tom said.

"How old are you?" Champlain asked.

"Almost sixteen, sir," Tom answered, standing his tallest. It was not very tall, but then Champlain himself was no taller.

"It might be worth trying," Champlain said, half to himself. "I'll think of it."

"Etienne is not much older than I. He goes everywhere with the Indians," Tom said. "And Nicholas does too."

"I'll think of it," Champlain repeated, then added, "I must see this Indian first and talk to him."

Champlain never learned to speak any of the Indian tongues. No doubt he understood some often-repeated words, but he had decided, he had told Tom, that as he evidently would never learn to speak well, he would not speak at all. It was better, he said, to say clearly in French what he had to say, to have his words well translated by an interpreter he trusted than to speak haltingly, perhaps using ridiculous words.

By "talking" to the Montagnais, he meant that the actual talking would be done by Tom. This left Champlain free to watch the Indians, both while they listened and while they spoke. He became very skillful at understanding the character of the Indians in this way but in these early days at Quebec, he made some mistakes and he made one now.

The Montagnais seemed to know the River of the Iroquois. He gave a description of the lake beyond it and its many islands that fitted well with what Moon Rises told them of the lake where her tribe would be. Actually the reason why the description fitted was that the Montagnais had heard Moon Rises talk about it. It was agreed that he should go in the canoe and have a hatchet when he started, another one, a kettle and a string of French beads when he and Tom and the canoe arrived safely back at Quebec.

The Indian never got his extra hatchet, the kettle or the beads. He went with the party until they reached the Lake of the Iroquois and had traveled some miles along its eastern shore. He helped cheerfully at the portages, steered skillfully past hidden rocks, caught trout in sunny pools, found dry wood for fires. The first night they camped on the lake shore, he got up silently while the others were sleeping.

The moon was shining on Tom's fair hair and on the fur of the white kittens curled up next to Small Arrow's dark head. Small Arrow had howled so at the idea of parting with his friends that they had taken them along. On the portages they both rode at Tom's belt in the same bag in which Minette had left France five years before.

The Indian looked longingly at Tom's hair. He balanced his hatchet thoughtfully in his hand for a moment. If there were an outcry the Iroquois might come. He had never meant from the first to let an Iroquois see him. Suppose there were some camped around the next point... He slung the pack containing their food and presents for Moon Rises' family over his shoulder and put the canoe on his head. A strong breeze blowing down the lake covered what noise he made and he made very little. He launched the canoe near where the lake narrows into the river. By the time Tom woke, Indian and canoe were gone and—as Membertou used to say—there is no trail in water.

He and Moon Rises both knew that they were too far from

Quebec to go back. They could only follow the trail that led south along the eastern shore of the lake, eating wild strawberries. Occasionally they stopped and fished. Once in a while they caught something. The Indian had taken their small supply of biscuit. He dared not go to Quebec, so when he reached the St. Lawrence he turned towards the great Rapids of La Chine.

There he traded the French goods he had stolen for furs with an Algonquin Indian who had come earlier to the trading fair. When the French traders came, they gave the Montagnais twice as many hatchets and kettles as he had had before. Thus he laid the basis for a solid business career. It was however a short one because the Algonquin found he had been cheated and killed him.

Before he died, the Montagnais had seen Etienne and had told him that Tom had been killed by the Iroquois, that Moon Rises and Small Arrow had gone back to their own tribe. No doubt Tom's scalp was the ornament of some Iroquois cabin, he said.

He told a most interesting story about how he had been hurrying to help his friends but had met a tall Iroquois in the moonlight. He even described how the Iroquois' face was painted. They had fought and the Iroquois fell under the blows of the French hatchet. He had only an old-fashioned stone axe, the Montagnais said with contempt.

By the time he had killed the Iroquois, Tom was dead, scalped. Moon Rises and the boy had vanished. He had then, not being anxious to meet more Iroquois, found the canoe where they had hidden it in the bushes and had stolen away as quickly as he could.

Along the lake of the Iroquois black flies and wild strawberries were beginning to appear. Moon Rises, Small Arrow and the kittens did not seem to interest the flies especially but Tom was bitten until his eyelids were so puffed that he could hardly see. He must have been a strange sight when he first met the Iroquois. Still they received him with courtesy and made many fine speeches, parts of which he could understand.

Before the speeches, they sat down with him in silence and passed him a pipe to smoke. This was the first time he had been given this sign of politeness and good will. He knew it was not necessary to smoke long. Tobacco was highly precious to the Indians and the less the visitor used, the more there was for the hosts. Tom took a small puff, succeeded in blowing the smoke out without choking and passed the pipe back.

The smoke burned in his throat and made him want to cough and sneeze. With his swollen face and stumbling way of speaking their tongue, he would, he knew, appear ridiculous in the eyes of these tall grave men. He choked down the cough and stopped the sneeze by pressing his cold fingers against the bridge of his nose. Tom never learned to like tobacco. "Perhaps," he used to say, "because the first time I tasted it, I was scared to death."

When they spoke, the Iroquois thanked him for bringing Moon Rises and Small Arrow back to their own people. Tom would always be their brother, they said. The chief, who was Moon Rises' brother, and her oldest son were away hunting but when they returned they would give a canoe and guides to take him back to the great River. They gave him at once, as Moon Rises had said they would, a belt decorated with beads and porcupine quills.

Then they all went fishing and Tom caught a four-foot gar-fish. It was a fierce and wicked-looking fish. Moon Rises told Tom that they had a way of sticking their snouts out of the water and pretending to be crooked sticks. Birds would light on them and the fish would then catch the birds and eat them. Tom did not exactly believe this story but he always looked carefully at old logs sticking out of the water. None of them was ever catching birds.

The Iroquois had their camp near the only grove of chestnut trees Tom had seen. Moon Rises showed him the prickly burs left over from the autumn before. She told him that when the leaves turned golden again there would be new burs packed full of nuts. They were good roasted in the ashes.

Tom suddenly felt homesick for the habitation on autumn nights, for his master sitting at the table near the fire, work-ing on his charts by candlelight, for French talk and French cooking and Etienne plucking his zither. He would even have been glad to see Nicholas Marsolet, though Nicholas was not a favorite of his. Nicholas lived with one of the Algonquin tribes now near Tadoussac and came with them to the trading fair at La Chine. It must be going on now, Tom thought, and wished he were on his way there in the canoe the Iroquois had promised him.

Without guides he could not manage one of the clumsy elm-bark canoes, he knew. He would only starve if he tried to go on foot. There was nothing to do until the chief returned and the tribe moved down the river to the St. Lawrence. He was treated as a guest but he knew he was really a prisoner. He belonged to the tribe the way the white cats did. Only they could run away and live in the woods like wildcats. He could not live like an Indian.

In the meantime this was his chance to learn their language. Its endless long words were beginning to have some meaning for him. With the young men of the tribe he sat in respectful silence while their elders discussed their hunting and fishing plans. He did not often see Moon Rises now. She was busy limping about her work with the other squaws but she always had a kind smile for Tom. Small Arrow would leave whatever mud puddle he was playing in, when he saw Tom, and run up to his friend purring. This was a great joke and even the tallest and most hideously painted braves would laugh over it.

Small Arrow often had a kitten, sometimes two in his arms. The kittens were given plenty of fish and they were growing large and handsome. Except for Tom they were probably the only inhabitants of the camp who washed their faces every day. Their white fur was spotless and their pink ears were like rose petals.

Was Minette their grandmother or their great-grandmother? Tom could not remember but he was glad to think that the green mountains he could see from the lake would always have white cats, descendants of Minette, in them. Tom tried to get Small Arrow to call the mountains *Monts Verts* but the closest the little Iroquois could come to it was Vermont. There was one mountain that looked like the profile of a very old Indian, so old that he had lost his teeth and his chin was higher than his nose. Another looked to Tom like a sleeping lion with his head on his paws. He told Small Arrow he could call it *Le Lion Couchant.*

They were paddling up the lake, Tom, Small Arrow and the cats—they were kittens no longer—in one of the big elm-bark canoes. Small Arrow had a paddle, not much bigger than a large spoon, which he dipped into the water with great energy. One of the braves, Hawk's Beak, was an old chief, an uncle of Moon Rises. The whole tribe had left their camp. Tom was disappointed that they were not going down the lake towards the St. Lawrence. Hawk's Beak told him that when the lake narrowed, they would cross to the Western shore. It was too wide here, he said. He told how the waves would rise with the wind and dash into the canoes, filling them with water and sinking them.

Tom remembered crossing from Iron Bound to Mount Desert and tried to tell Hawk's Beak about it but the old man only grunted. He'd rather talk about his own travels, Tom thought. Well, I can learn more by listening than by talking.

He learned many things by listening to Hawk's Beak—about the Five Nations of his people who lived west of the lake, behind those blue mountains. He called them the Adirondacks. His people used the eastern side of the lake for their hunting ground, he said. Sometimes the Algonquins came there but the Iroquois chased them away. He added that the Iroquois always won the battles because they were braver and stronger than the Algonquins. Their canoes were stronger than those birch-bark things. Their medicine men were wiser.

The Algonquins, he said, were a lot of squaws. His opinion of the Hurons was also poor. They did not grow their own tobacco or catch their own beaver. They were only traders who would travel forty days to cheat someone out of a beaver skin. What sort of work was that for a man?

He showed Tom two scalps, one Huron, one Algonquin, that hung from his belt. He had never had a French scalp, he said. Tom felt that prickling in his blond hair again.

Chapter 7

TICONDEROGA

Early that June, Champlain went down to Tadoussac to meet Pontgravé. The terrible winter had left only eight Frenchmen alive at the habitation. Etienne and Nicholas were two of them. Even Champlain himself had been ill with scurvy though he recovered when he ate green shoots of a tree called annedda that the Indians showed him.

He was sad about the deaths of so many of the colonists, especially so about having allowed Tom Lee to go on his mission to the Iroquois. Not a day passed without his missing Tom. Still he was not discouraged about the future of Canada. He had plans for trade and discovery about which he talked with Pontgravé.

"Ever since the Algonquins saw a Frenchman bring down a moose with a bullet from an arquebus, they have been asking us to use those thunder tubes against their enemies," Champlain said. "We promised them ten months ago that we would help them. It is time that we kept our promises. The Indians will not respect us if we do not keep them and we cannot explore farther west without their aid. I must go with them against the Iroquois."

Pontgravé roared out his agreement. He had gout and his swollen foot was resting on a stool.

"I'd go with you if there were a canoe strong enough so I wouldn't sink it," he shouted. "Lame foot and all, I'd go. They'd find out what I think of savages who would murder a boy like Tom Lee. A good boy, if I ever saw one. A fine Norman boy—a real Malouin!"

Champlain did not remind Pontgravé that Tom was half English and half southern French. He only said gravely, "He is a great loss to me and to the colony. He would have made one of my best interpreters. As good as Jean Nicolet. As good as Etienne. Better perhaps in some ways."

Pontgravé also agreed with Champlain that the barques belonging to the trading company should meet the Indian canoes near the foot of the La Chine rapids, to save their friends a long journey and the danger of passing the River of the Iroquois. It would also, as Champlain had pointed out, make it more difficult for the Basque fur traders to do business with the Indians than if the trading were carried on farther down the river. The Basques did not belong to the fur company but they took advantage of the friendship between Champlain and the Indians. Furs intended for de Monts' company often went back to France in Basque ships.

Pontgravé made a few uncomplimentary remarks about the Basques. "They are worse than the Iroquois," he roared. "Thieves! Scoundrels!"

After a time he calmed down enough so that they could

make their plans. Champlain left Tadoussac the next day, sailing with the tide up the river in a shallop with twenty men. One of them was Etienne, who went as an interpreter. They passed the habitation two days later but did not stop there. It looked cool and peaceful in the shadow of the great rock with pigeons fluttering around the dovecotes and a white rose Champlain had brought from France blooming in his garden. Jean Nicolet, the best of the interpreters, joined them there.

Beyond Three Rivers they met more than two hundred Hurons and Algonquins. The Hurons were the finest-looking Indians Champlain had ever seen. Their name came from the way they wore their hair. It was shaved so that there was only a narrow pad of bristles on top of their heads. A Frenchman who saw this bristly brush had exclaimed, "Quelles Hures!" meaning "What wild boars!" The name had grown into Hurons and had stuck to them ever since.

"They were," Champlain wrote in his journal, "ready to help us in our discoveries in the country of the Iroquois with whom they are in mortal conflict and they spare nothing belonging to these enemies."

The Huron chief, Ochateguin, an Algonquin, Chief Iroquet, and Champlain met and exchanged presents. For a long time the Indians smoked in silence. Then Iroquet, with Nicolet translating for him, said that many months ago Champlain had promised to help them against their enemies. Now he, Iroquet, had brought the Hurons to meet the French, whom they had a great wish to see. The Hurons, he said, were warriors of great courage. They knew the trails and lakes of the Iroquois country and they would show them to the French.

Champlain thanked him and said that he was ready to start with the chiefs to help them against their enemies.

"But first," said Iroquet, "we would like to visit the wonderful house of the Men of Iron at Quebec. We would like to hear the thunder tubes speak."

Champlain at once had arquebuses and muskets fired and all the Indians shouted in astonishment. Then they all went back to Quebec and there was almost a week of feasting and dancing. To Champlain the tramp of dancing feet, the war songs and the yelling seemed endless. However, the rejoicing was over at last and they started up the river again. They crossed Lac St. Pierre and arrived at the mouth of the River of the Iroquois.

Here a number of Indians, including some especially warlike dancers, decided to take the French goods they had received for their furs and go home. Champlain and nine Frenchmen in the shallop and many Indians in canoes went on up the Iroquois River. The Indians told Champlain that he could sail all the way to the Lake of the Iroquois, a beautiful lake with many fine islands in it and mountains on both sides. Unfortunately there were rapids in the way and a waterfall so steep that the shallop could not possibly go up it. The woods around the fall were so thick that they could not drag the shallop through them. Champlain, however, decided to go in a canoe. He had two reasons. He was determined to carry out his promise to his Indian friends and he wanted to see the lake where the Iroquois lived. Perhaps it, rather than the rapids he called La Chine, might be the road to the Pacific.

He called for volunteers to go with him. Only two stepped forward. The others went back to Quebec in the shallop.

"Their noses bled," Champlain wrote of these cowards.

By the 12th of July, 1609, they had passed the rapids and the steep waterfall. They held a review above the fall. There were sixty Indians in twenty-five canoes: Hurons, Montagnais, some Algonquins from the Ottawa River. The Indians were painted in a dizzy array of colors and patterns. They were armed with bows and arrows, spears and clubs. Some of them had French axes, some carried stone ones. They wore almost no clothes yet seemed not to be troubled by black flies and mosquitoes.

The three Frenchmen with their steel armor worn over heavy clothes and their plumed helmets were a strange contrast to the Indians. Their baggage was heavy—their arquebuses with the powder and bullets for them, their swords, Champlain's bronze astrolabe, their biscuit and salt beef. It all grew heavier still as they carried it on the portages with their escort of black flies.

Champlain marveled at the skill with which the Indians managed their canoes and the speed with which they built their shelters for the night. They would draw up their canoes on the bank of the river, build wigwams and chop down trees for a barricade almost before the French had unloaded their canoe and stacked their weapons, covering them from the dampness. One of the three Frenchmen always kept careful watch over the pile, so they could arm themselves quickly in case the enemy appeared.

It was, Champlain knew, just as important to watch their friends. Any of them would have liked a chance to disappear in the woods with one of the magic thunder tubes.

The Indians never kept watch after they had built their barricade. By day they sent scouts ahead both by land and by water. When these reported that they had seen no Iroquois, they all went to sleep. Champlain tried to explain to them that they ought to take turns being on guard like the French. The Indians replied that they worked hard by day and liked to sleep at night. At least their snores helped to keep Champlain awake while he was watching over the sleeping camp.

There was always a special wigwam covered with beaver skins for the medicine man. Before the Indians went to sleep, he would go into his wigwam and talk to a special stone he had. He claimed it answered his questions. After he had asked the stone for information, he would seize a pole of the wigwam with his teeth and shake it until the whole thing seemed about to fall. Mutterings and grunts and different voices, some high, some low, would follow. At last he would come out and tell them where the enemy were and how many there were of them. Also how many of them the allies would kill. The Indians would squat around the tent listening solemnly to what Champlain told them was nonsense. They politely paid no attention to him.

After the medicine man had given his information, the chiefs would drill the warriors. They would give each man a stick and take longer ones themselves. Then they would level off a piece of ground and arrange the sticks on it in a pattern, arranging themselves in the same pattern. When they learned what it was, they would fall out of the pattern and mix themselves up, then at a signal take the same position again, all with great speed and without confusion.

During the day when the scouts and hunters went ashore, they would visit certain trees where they might find signs of friends or enemies. The hunters would bring in food—a deer, wild geese, perhaps a bear. When there was food, they ate it all. When there was none, they cheerfully went without.

Suddenly, one hot evening, the river broadened out into a beautiful lake with the long summer twilight still shining on it. This was the lake where they would find their enemies, the Indians said. Now they must hide by day and travel only by night.

This meant slow going. It was not until July 29th that at last they met the Iroquois. Champlain and his Indian allies had almost reached the end of the lake by then. They had crossed to the western side and were paddling quietly along the edge of a rounded cape. Etienne told Champlain that the Indians called it Ticonderoga.

Suddenly from the other side of the cape they heard shouts and cries and the sound of heavy canoes splashing through the water. A band of Iroquois was moving towards them in their heavy elm-bark canoes. Their scouts must have seen Champlain's party and reported it because the Iroquois were already heading for the shore. They knew that their canoes could not be managed so well as the light birch-bark canoes of the allies. Soon the elm-bark canoes were hauled up on the shore and there came the sound of trees being chopped down for a barricade.

"They used," Champlain wrote, "their stone axes and the poor axes they sometimes win in war."

His party stayed on the water, lashing their canoes together with long poles. When the barricade was built, two Iroquois canoes left the shore and paddled out towards the allies.

"Do you come to make war on us?" the Iroquois asked.

Chief Ochateguin replied courteously, "We have no other desire than to fight with you but for the moment nothing can be done. We must have daylight."

"Very well," replied the Iroquois, "we will wait for sunrise and then attack you."

Ochateguin agreed and the Iroquois paddled back to their barricade.

All night there was dancing and yelling on shore. On the water the allies sang songs in which they insulted their enemies and boasted of their own courage. Both sides bragged that they would have victory in the morning. Champlain slept through much of this boasting. He woke at dawn when the allies landed. They carefully concealed the three Frenchmen from the enemy. Champlain sent the other two into the woods with orders to make a wide circle and get on the far side of the Iroquois within arquebus range. He himself was well hidden by the tall Hurons. Even the plumes on his helmet only came up to their shoulders.

The allies took the positions they had practiced so often with the sticks. The Iroquois marched out from the barricade in equally good order.

There must have been two hundred, Champlain figured. They were tall, strong, fine-looking men. They marched slowly with great gravity and calm. Three chiefs at the head looked even taller than the others because of the high plumes they wore on their heads.

Chief Iroquet made a sign to Champlain that the time had come to do what he could against them. Champlain was ready to use what courage and skill he had.

The allies started running and traveled swiftly two hundred yards towards the Iroquois. They stood firm. They saw neither Champlain nor the two Frenchmen hiding in the woods. Now Iroquet and Ochateguin called with loud cries. The allies divided into two groups.

"My place," Champlain wrote later, "was twenty yards ahead and I marched on between two lines of our allies till I was thirty yards from the enemy. They halted and gazed at me and I at them. When I saw them raise their bows to shoot, I took aim at one of the chiefs with my arquebus. I had put four bullets in it. I shot straight at him. He and the next man to him fell to the ground, dead. Another was wounded and died later. Our people shouted so loud you could not have heard thunder. Neither they nor the Iroquois could tell how it was that the bullets went through the Iroquois shields, which are thickly woven of sticks and thread. As I reloaded my arquebus, I heard my companions firing from the woods. This frightened the Iroquois so that they took flight."

A few got away in canoes. Many escaped into the woods. Several were killed by the Indians. Some of the allies were wounded by arrows but the wounds soon healed. The Iroquois left everything in the fort—cornmeal, bear meat, arrows, skins of bear and beaver and, securely lashed to the barricade, Thomas Godfrey Lee.

CHAPTER 8

CAPE VICTORY

IN THE feasting and dancing that followed the fight at Ticonderoga the two quietest people were the happiest. Champlain with his own hands had cut the thongs that bound Tom to the barricades.

Neither said that he was glad to see the other. They knew it without speaking.

"They have not hurt you?" Champlain asked.

"No. It was only to keep me from running away," Tom said. "They have been kind to me. Because of Moon Rises and Small Arrow, you know."

"Do you know what happened to them?"

"The chiefs sent the women and children to the east side of the lake last night. Small Arrow had the cats in his arms. Just as the canoes were leaving he had run back for them. I think Moon Rises would have set me free if she had not been hurried away. I hope they are safe in what Small Arrow calls Vermont. It is his way of saying Green Mountains."

"He speaks French?" Champlain asked smiling.

"Better than I speak Iroquois," Tom said. "But I suppose he will soon forget," he added rather sadly. "Still, I like to think that there will always be white cats in Vermont."

The yelling and shrieking of the Indians went on and on. Their dancing feet trampled the grass down into hard bare ground. Smoke poured from fires, the first they had lighted in many days. There was a smell of deer meat cooking in their precious French kettles. They made *sagamité*, a thin cornmeal mush with pieces of tough leathery meat and whole fish with the scales still on. Sometimes they added blueberries.

It was considered a great delicacy, Tom told his master as Champlain accepted a full porringer from one of the chiefs.

"Do you remember the Good Time Order, sir?" Tom asked.

"Only too well," Champlain said.

He had tasted the *sagamité*.

He and Tom were still awake when all the Indians had stuffed and danced themselves into snoring sleep. Champlain told Tom about the battle and Tom told about his journey.

"Sleep, Thomas. I will keep watch," Champlain said at last. The Iroquois might come again. I will write a little in my notebook and draw a picture of the battle and a map of the lake. Go to sleep."

"Yes, but wake me so that I can take the next watch, sir. You are right about a night attack. Half the stories they tell around the fires are about men being surprised in their sleep and killed."

He lay awake for a while watching his master's pen turn and twist in the light from a lantern. It was like being in the habitation again. He thought back to all the places he had seen

Champlain writing and drawing—at Quebec, Port Royal, St. Croix, in the cabin of the ship.

When he woke it was dawn and Champlain was working on his chart.

Tom looked down at the map with its islands. The shape of it had never been so clear to him before.

"You should call it Lake Champlain," he said.

"With the King's permission, perhaps," Champlain answered, but he wrote on the chart "Lake of the Iroquois."

He wished to explore farther south. The Indians told him of another lake. They showed him its outlet and said that there was a big river to the south that would take him to Norumbega. They would guide him there some day, they said, but now they would go no farther. They must take their prisoners and their Iroquois scalps and go home.

The Indians traveled north rapidly, stopping occasionally to hunt and to torture their prisoners. Tom had seen Indian scalps many times but he had never known what happened to a man before he was scalped. To him and to Champlain it was a shock to learn what cruelty lived in these savages hand in hand with their patience, cheerfulness and kindness.

The first man the Hurons tortured was told to sing as they tore out his nails and burned him. Neither Champlain nor Tom could eat the food that was cooking on the same fire where the hatchets were heating.

"He sang," Champlain wrote later in his notebook, "but it was a sad song to hear."

Champlain saw nothing amusing in the jokes that went on

but the prisoner was supposed to laugh. He was a young man but as he was brave, they respectfully called him "Uncle" as they burned him with the heated axes.

One Indian would say, "My uncle is cold. I must warm him a little." Another would add, "My uncle is a canoe. Ah, this canoe is not strong. It needs more pitch. Is the pitch hot enough, Uncle? Is it good?"

"Yes, it is fine pitch and very hot," the prisoner said smiling.

He never groaned or cried out.

When the Hurons asked Champlain to join in the sport, he could bear it no longer.

"Tell them," he said to Thomas, "that I will not do this evil work. I will, however, kill him with my arquebus if he must be killed."

The Indians liked to kill their prisoners as slowly as possible but as a special favor to Champlain they allowed him to shoot the unfortunate Iroquois with his arquebus. So this particular misery was ended. Champlain had seen suffering and cruelty in his life but never such delight in both. He saw what it might mean to anger his savage allies. He realized that he would never have authority over them. They never obeyed even their own chiefs unless it suited them to do so.

The only way to win their respect was by courage, patience, courtesy and by faithfulness to a promise. Luckily these things were all part of Champlain's nature. He became known among the Indians as one who kept his word when others broke theirs, as going into danger when others turned back. Along miles of forest trails where he had never set foot he became known as Champlain Renowned for Valor. When the

Hurons and Algonquins turned towards their own country, they called him their brother and invited him to come to visit them and again to help them against their enemies. This he promised to do.

With the Montagnais, traveling sixty miles a day, he went on to Tadoussac to celebrate the victory. The Indians announced it to their friends on shore by beating their paddles against their canoes and yelling all together, one echoing shout for each prisoner they had brought. Each man who had a scalp waved it from the end of his paddle. The women swam out from shore, snatched the scalps off the paddles and hung them round their necks. When the men landed, both they and the women danced and sang for hours.

It was a relief to Champlain to get back to the habitation at Quebec and see that everything was in order for the winter—that there was plenty of food in the storehouse, that the roofs did not leak, that there was enough powder and shot for winter hunting. Champlain would have liked to stay at Quebec but he had to go back to France and report to de Monts and to the King on the affairs of the fur company.

The voyage was a good one. Pontgravé had made the trip so often that he said the ship could find the way blindfolded to a good Norman harbor in six weeks or less. This year they left on September 5th and reached Honfleur on October 15th.

Tom was left at Quebec to act as interpreter for the Sieur du Pare, who was in command there. He helped his master pack up the presents he was taking to the King. There was the snout of a five-foot garfish, an Iroquois scalp from the Montagnais—the squaws had trimmed it with beads—and a belt decorated with porcupine quills. There were also two scarlet tanagers, which Champlain called "little birds of a carnation color."

The King was glad to see his old companion in arms again and he treated him kindly but the days seemed long to Champlain until it was time to sail to Canada again. Spring came early in 1610. Fishermen who had been visiting the Grand Banks for many years said it was the earliest spring they had heard of since Cartier's time. The ship arrived at Tadoussac on May 26th and Champlain was soon at Quebec.

Fruit trees were white all through the woods along the St. Lawrence, whiter than the steaming curtain of water at Montmorency Falls. On the big island across from the falls, the meadows were full of flowers. Even the rock above the habitation shone that morning against a sky with great sailing, shining clouds. The waving blue and white flag with the lilies of France was bright against the gray rock.

They could see men running across the drawbridge and down to the waterside. Champlain saw a quick-moving Indian dash towards one of the cannon. He noticed with a smile that the Indian had blond hair. There was a puff of smoke and the Indian vanished. Then Champlain saw him again, down on the wharf, almost before the roar of salute died away. He was yelling like a real Indian in answer to Pontgravé's shout of "Malouins." They had had a fine winter, Tom told his master later. Hunting had been good. There was little scurvy. Champlain wrote in his notebook that, as he had hoped, there was less scurvy when a colony did not depend on salt provisions than when salt food must be eaten.

He was pleased with the look of the habitation. His roses

were alive. Peas were coming up. He would have liked to stay and work among his roses but he had only a short time at Quebec. Sixty Montagnais warriors, on their way to fight the Iroquois, came to the habitation. Tom was soon telling his master, "They say there are Basque traders and Mistigoches—that is what they call the Normans—up the river. They say these traders have promised to help them fight their enemies. They want you to say if you think the Basque traders will really fight."

"Tell them no," Champlain said. "All they want is their furs."

The Indians burst out laughing.

"They are women," they shouted. "They make war on beaver skins! But will you help us?"

"Ask them if I have ever failed in a promise to them," Champlain said.

Shouting Champlain's praises and scorn of Mistigoches and Basques, the Indians set off up the river. Champlain followed in a barque. At Three Rivers an Algonquin messenger met them. He pulled a piece of copper a foot long out of a sack and gave it to Champlain. It came from a lake near where the sun set, he said. Chief Iroquet had sent it. He was on his way with four hundred Hurons and two hundred of his own men. They would meet Champlain at the mouth of the Iroquois River.

The Basque fur traders were anchored near Three Rivers. By this time the Montagnais were circling around the barques in their canoes, shouting to the traders to keep their promises and help them against the Iroquois. The traders made many excuses for not going and the Montagnais paddled off again shouting that the traders were woman-hearted and made war only on furs.

The Hurons reached the mouth of the Iroquois River before Champlain and set off for the battle without waiting for him. When he arrived a messenger came hurrying to meet him.

"A hundred Indians are barricaded in a fort," he said. "We have attacked them but they are too strong for us. Some of us are wounded. You are our only hope. Come quickly!"

The Montagnais seized their bows, spears and shields. They hurried on so fast that Champlain was left behind. Only five Frenchmen volunteered to go with him and they were so weighted down with their armor and their weapons that they made slow progress. However, they followed the track the Montagnais had taken, wading up to their knees in mud, tormented by mosquitoes, until at last they heard the noise of battle.

From behind their barricade, the Iroquois were shouting insults at the allies. Like the Hurons, the Montagnais had attacked the fort and been thrown back.

The fort was circular in shape, strongly made of tree trunks interlaced with branches. As Champlain moved towards it to see where to attack, an arrow from the fort pierced the lobe of his ear and went through into his neck. He tore out the arrow and went on. Tom, who was binding up the leg of a bleeding Huron, was struck by an arrow in the arm. Champlain tore it out of Tom's arm as he passed him. They both went on with what they were doing. The arrow was tipped with a sharp stone, Tom noticed. He carried the wounded Huron into the woods and went back to his master. Champlain, still with blood running down his neck, was surrounded by several chiefs and was trying to tell them by signs what to do.

He turned gladly to Tom and said, "Tell them to go forward

under cover of their shields and attach ropes to those two posts. While they do this, we will fire on the Iroquois and keep them from shooting. Then, when I shout, our friends must pull at once on the ropes. The barricade will fall. We can all rush in."

The Indians followed his orders swiftly. The French kept the Iroquois off with musket fire, killing several. The Indians attached the ropes to the posts, as Champlain had commanded.

A short time before, on one of the Norman barques, a young man called Des Prairies had heard the sounds of the battle. He said to his fellow sailors, "It is a shame to let the Sieur de Champlain fight the Indians alone."

He came in his shallop with several men and arrived in time to see the Indians haul on the posts and break down the barricade. So many Iroquois had been killed or wounded by bullets from arquebuses and muskets that the men remaining in the fort were terrified. When the gap was made by pulling down the posts, the Montagnais and Hurons swarmed in. All the Iroquois were either killed or taken prisoner. Champlain called the place Cap de la Victoire—Cape Victory. When he drew a picture of the battle he took care to show Des Prairies' shallop in it.

Three of the allies were killed and forty wounded. Tom was busy bandaging wounds, including his own. The Indians were pleased with their decorations but Champlain would not consent to have his ear bandaged. It had stopped bleeding and would heal well enough, he said.

"Did you kill anyone, gosling?" Etienne asked, boasting that he had killed three Iroquois himself.

"No," said Tom. "I pointed my gun once but I—I couldn't pull the trigger," he added honestly.

Etienne clapped him on the shoulder, not unkindly.

"Oh, well, we need you to pick up the pieces," he said.

Tom wished there were no pieces to pick up. He hated killing and the taking of scalps and the tortures that followed a battle. The Indians would call him woman-hearted, he supposed.

Yet they did not do so. They knew it was not cowardice that made Champlain ask them not to torture their prisoners, not cowardice either that made it impossible for Tom Lee to kill Iroquois. Champlain was their Man of Iron, their friend. Tom was their friend too. They were accustomed to his yellow hair, to his bright blue eyes and sunburned nose. They called him Two Tongues and Medicine Man who Binds Wounds. They spoke to him kindly, telling him he would always be welcome in their battles. They would scalp his enemies for him, they said. They gave him a new headband, handsomely beaded and trimmed with moose hair dyed crimson and three beaver skins.

They pointed out to him that the skins were clean and had been taken off the backs of beavers, not from Iroquois. They said this in mockery of the Basque traders who, as soon as the battle was over, had rushed into the fort, tearing bloodstained furs off dead Iroquois.

"Did we not say they made war only on furs?" they shouted as they started home after painting on their canoes a head for each Iroquois killed.

Chief Iroquet and his Algonquins arrived too late for the battle. They brought furs to trade. The Basques and Normans got most of them. Champlain had faced all the dangers. The traders carried off the profit.

"We did them a great favor," Champlain wrote—and planned new journeys. He was determined to learn of the great lake far to the west where the copper came from. The Indians called it an inland sea. Yes, they said, it might be salt. It might well be a bay of the Pacific and the way to China, Champlain thought. Later he learned that when the Indians did not know the answer to a question, they gave him the one they thought he would like best.

The idea that the lake with copper on it might be part of the Pacific excited him greatly. Since it was time for him to return to France, he decided to ask Chief Iroquet to take Etienne Brulé with him for the winter. Iroquet, though he was an Algonquin, often spent the winter in the Huron country. Etienne would be able to learn both languages and find out about the lake, perhaps even visit its coppery shores.

After a good deal of talk between Iroquet and Champlain, the chief agreed to take Etienne with him. Champlain took in exchange a young Huron, son of a Huron chief, whom he called Savignon. With Champlain also went Tom Lee for his first visit to France in six years.

CHAPTER 9

PARIS—FRANCE

THEY LEFT Quebec on August 8th, 1610, and arrived in Honfleur on September 27th. Savignon proved to be an excellent traveler. He liked the great swarms of sea birds. He marveled at Ile Percée, that tall rock archway through which a boat can pass. He was not frightened when, in midocean, the ship seemed to strike a rock. They had passed over a sleeping whale, Tom told Savignon, who danced on deck in excitement and wanted to chase the whale in a canoe. Later he went whale-fishing with the sailors, learned to throw a harpoon and to like whale steak, broiled fresh. He climbed the rigging and reefed sails when gales were blowing. He learned to speak French better than Tom did Huron. It was the desire of his heart to own a beaver hat.

The journey to Paris in a coach with four horses was a wonderful adventure to Savignon. Cattle in the fields, flocks of sheep, hens around the door of a stone cottage, all were marvels.

For Champlain it was a sad journey. A rumor he had heard at Tadoussac proved to be true. His master, his fellow soldier, his good friend Henry the Fourth had been killed by an assassin. His son Louis the Thirteenth, a small boy only nine years old, was now the King.

King Louis was making snowballs in the garden of the Louvre, his palace, when Tom and Savignon saw him. Snow, so common in Canada, was rare in Paris. The weather had been foggy and rainy so far. Savignon was delighted with the snow and raced through the streets so fast that Tom could hardly keep up with him.

"You are like a wild moose!" Tom told him.

Tom was supposed to keep Savignon out of mischief. He found him making a snowball to throw at the King. He scowled furiously when Tom told him he must not do it.

"He threw one at me," he said.

"I will not lend you my beaver hat to wear to the wedding," Tom said. "See if you can hit that pigeon."

The snowball almost hit the pigeon and did hit the roof of the Louvre.

"Come home and try on the hat," Tom said.

The wedding was Champlain's. It had been arranged between him and Hélène Boullé, daughter of one of the court secretaries. This was the day the contracts were going to be signed. The bride was only twelve years old. The contracts provided that she remain with her parents for two years. The wedding ceremony took place several days later in the church of St. Germain facing the Louvre.

Savignon and Tom, both fashionably dressed in French clothes, were among the wedding guests. Tom wore his own beaver hat. Champlain, seeing Savignon prancing around in Tom's hat, lent Savignon his old hat. He had a new one for the wedding. Tom liked him in the old one best, the one that had been on the table six years before when he first saw his master. There were a few spots of ink on it because it had so often been beside Champlain when he was writing. Champlain had a new ribbon put on it for Savignon instead of the battered old feathers that had been its ornament for so long. In his new red coat Savignon was the most gaily dressed member of the wedding party.

The bride was a pretty little fair-haired girl. She was shy with the grandly dressed court ladies who came to the wedding breakfast but she was not afraid of Savignon with his coppery skin, darting black eyes and the straight black hair that looked so strange under the beaver hat. It was only at first with the greatest difficulty that Tom got Savignon to take the hat off in church and in the house.

"I feel as if I lost my scalp," he said.

However, he watched what the court gentlemen did with their beavers and was soon sweeping his off as gracefully as anyone.

For a few weeks after the wedding, Champlain with Tom and Savignon would call for Hélène and all four would go walking to see the sights of Paris. They saw dancing bears. They listened to street musicians. They watched jugglers. They did not realize that they—Champlain, Tom and Savignon with Hélène skipping along beside them—were one of the sights of the town.

One evening there was a display of fireworks that spangled the sky with colored stars and made Savignon jump and howl like a catamount. It was the King's birthday. In the morning

they had seen him ride out through the palace gates in a gilded coach drawn by eight horses. Savignon loved the coach.

"Perhaps the King will know me and take me to ride with him," he said but the King had already learned to bow graciously to his subjects without seeing them.

"He didn't see me. He didn't see my hat," Savignon said sadly.

He had soon forgotten his disappointment. There was so much to see. He loved to look up at the tall steeples and listen to the church bells. Even better, he liked a clock in Champlain's lodgings. It talked all the time, he said, and it told him when it was time to go to the cookshop for dinner. Savignon liked beef cooked with onions and spice and wine. He liked his soft bed. He liked the shop signs—a gilded boot, a painted clock with hands always at twenty minutes past eight, a key two feet long.

However, he was scornful of the Frenchmen he sometimes saw quarreling in the streets.

"They talk too much," he said to Tom, "but they never strike a blow or kill each other. They are cowards."

"Say it in Huron," Tom said hastily and Savignon called out that they were women and would never take scalps if they did not show more courage.

He groaned loudly when Tom told him that they were leaving Paris and France and going back to Canada. He did not wish to lead that hard life with those savages, he said, but they sailed with Pontgravé on the first of March, 1611.

It was a bad voyage. There were drifting mountains of ice, bigger fields of it than even Pontgravé had ever seen. Champlain described in his journal various narrow escapes from drifting bergs and ice floes, and wrote, with his usual moderation: "These frequent encounters with the ice annoyed us somewhat."

They did not reach Tadoussac for two and a half months. There were Basque traders there already but, as Champlain wrote: "These people are mistaken who think that by coming early they can get the best furs. The Indians are too sharp and crafty. Where they used to sell a beaver for two knives, they now want a dozen. They keep their furs for more customers and higher prices."

The Basque traders knew that Champlain must have promised to meet his Huron and Algonquin friends. They watched him constantly to see whether he would start up the river or whether the meeting would be at Tadoussac. Champlain managed to slip away from them and reach Quebec ahead of them. All was well there. He went on towards the great La Chine rapids.

When they reached the rapids there were no Indians there to meet them.

"We will go downstream," Champlain said, "and decide where to build a trading post."

The fast-moving river carried them swiftly to the island where Cartier had found the Indian settlement of Hochelaga. Here, below the steep slopes of the mountain Cartier had named Mount Royal, were the kind of meadows Champlain loved. Cattle could graze there, he said. Wild plum and cherry were in bloom, so fruit trees would grow there. The ground was white with wild strawberry blossoms.

He called a beautiful spot close to the river Place Royale. He named a small island Ile de Sainte Hélène for his wife. He had his men clear land for a garden. They made bricks of clay they found and built a wall around it. Champlain himself sowed the seeds.

At last the Algonquins and Hurons arrived at the rapids. Tom and Savignon went with Champlain to meet them. Savignon wore his red coat and—Champlain had given it to him for his own—his beaver hat. They watched eagerly for familiar faces as canoes came shooting down through the green and white water and landed on a gently sloping beach a little upstream from where they were standing, but they saw no one they knew.

Then a voice from behind them said, "Introduce me to your friend from Paris, gosling."

Tom spun around. Etienne slipped out from behind a white birch and stood grinning at him. His face was painted with streaks of white, yellow and red. Between the stripes his skin was almost as dark as an Indian's. His black hair had strips of beaded deerskin twisted into it. He was naked to the waist. His clothes were Indian breeches of white doeskin, beautifully decorated moccasins and the rattlesnake belt Tom remembered. The rattles hung around his neck, not on a plain leather thong but from a collar of beads and porcupine quills. He moved like an Indian, quietly, swiftly. He even, Tom noticed, smelled like an Indian—greasy, fishy, smoky, slightly sweet.

The French bow he made to Champlain looked strange. It sounded strange too because it set the rattles quivering with the dry whirring noise that is like no other sound. He answered Champlain's questions courteously. Yes, the Indians had treated him well. Yes, he had improved his Algonquin speech. No, he had not learned much Huron yet, it was most difficult. Yes, he could explain why the Indians had not come to trade until now. It was because of a rumor.

It was extraordinary, Tom thought, how news and false rumors could travel so swiftly through endless miles of empty forest, up rushing streams, around roaring falls, along twisting trails. This particular rumor was that Savignon had died in Paris, that Champlain had made an alliance with the Iroquois, that he and six hundred Iroquois were waiting for the Hurons and Algonquins at the rapids to make war on them. So most of the allies had not come to trade.

"But," said Etienne, "I persuaded Chief Iroquet that the news could not be true. So he has come with his men and a few Hurons. They invite you to smoke and talk with them."

Then Chief Iroquet, the Huron Chief Ochateguin and Savignon's brother Tregourati came out of the woods. The Frenchmen in Champlain's shallop fired their arquebuses in the air for a salute. The Indians shouted almost louder than the gunfire. The Basque traders arrived in their shallops. There were thirteen of them. They fired off their guns too and the Indians were frightened.

"They ask you to let them make no more such thunderings," Savignon said. "They think the Basques mean to do them harm."

"Tell them," said Champlain, "that we are all the servants of one King and that we are all their friends."

The Indians who came to parley with Champlain brought him a hundred beaver skins. They received French hatchets in exchange. With Etienne translating for the Algonquins and

Savignon for the Hurons, they answered Champlain's questions about the country to the west.

Four of them claimed that they had been as far as the Western Ocean. They said the water was salt. Tom, watching their faces and listening, thought that this was one of the times when the answers were based on what they knew Champlain would like to hear. They told of a great river by which their friends reached Florida and the salt sea and of another further west that led to another salt sea. Their talk was confusing perhaps because Savignon did not understand the questions.

Tom was with his master at several meetings with the Indians. They still feared that the traders would attack them. They always repeated that Champlain was their friend, that they would show him their country, that they would be happy if he would build his house near theirs. He said many times that he would always be their friend, that he would ask the King to give him soldiers to help them in their wars and also priests to help them to be Christians.

The Indians were still afraid of the Basques. They stole away from the wigwams and barricade they had built near the rapids and went to the Lake of the Two Mountains which the shallops could not reach. From there they sent Savignon, who had gone with them rather unwillingly, beaver hat and all, to ask Champlain to meet them privately. He took Tom with him. They went on shore along the rapids of La Chine. The water slid past them with quiet swiftness, boiling up here and there in white foam, sometimes leaping down three feet at a time in a green and white cataract, sometimes calm and blue. Yet even in the quiet places, a chip thrown into the stream traveled so fast that it soon vanished from sight.

They had to go miles through the woods before they found the lake and the Indian camp. They were greeted with the usual shouts of welcome. Savignon told them that meat and fish were on the fire, being broiled the way Champlain liked them. While the food was cooking, Savignon entertained his friends with stories about Paris.

"The King," he said, "is a small boy no taller than a heron. He rides in a rolling cabin made of gold. It is drawn by eight moose without horns."

His hearers doubled up, laughing.

"At night," Savignon went on, "he had the sky filled with stars of fire—red, blue and green. They are rainbows that speak like thunder. He has a servant shut up in a box that speaks to him, tells the King when it is time for dinner. Like this—ding, ding, ding..."

Savignon imitated a clock striking twelve times. His friends laughed some more. They asked him if it was true that French-women all had beards. Savignon said no, that their skin was as smooth as a young squaw's. The Indians shook their heads in disbelief.

"Nicholas de Vignau told us so. He is French. He knows better than you."

Nicholas was a fat-faced, fat-fisted young man who had come to the rapids in one of the Basque shallops.

"He's a liar," Savignon said. "I tell you I have seen Paris and I know. The bears there wear red coats and breeches and dance like Hurons," he added.

"Why do you try to make fools of us with such stories?" his brother asked.

"His hat has crushed his brain and made him mad," shouted another.

Poor Savignon!

It did no good for Tom to tell them that Savignon spoke the truth. It only made them think that he too was trying to make fools of them.

"Perhaps," he told Savignon, "it would be better not to talk so much of Paris," but Savignon went right on talking about it.

"Do you remember," he asked, "how we ate trout with lemon and butter and parsley in that warm little shop in the Street of the Bear? And the little tarts full of cream and strawberry jam? No one here knows how to cook. Madame de Champlain was learning how to make pastry. I would like a French wife. Do you think I could buy one for three beaver skins? I have two."

Tom, who was having difficulty keeping his face straight, answered that a French wife was expensive and would not work so hard as an Indian wife.

Savignon still thought he would like a French one.

"She could easily learn," he said, "to get wood for the fires, make moccasins and snowshoes and fishnets, smooth shells into wampum, skin a moose and carry the meat. All young women learn these things from the wise old women of the tribe, also to make papoose boards and dance when the papoose cries and make leggings and robes of deerskin. But to make pastry. That must be learned in France."

He looked sad when he finally said goodbye to Champlain

and Tom and left in his brother's canoe for the journey up the Ottawa River.

He said to Tom, "It is a hard life I am going to lead," and repeated that he would give three beaver skins, perhaps four or even five, for a French wife.

Nicholas de Vignau, who was going with the Algonquins up the Ottawa, jeered: "He has no beaver except his hat—and he has forgotten how to catch them!"

Tom thought Nicholas de Vignau was almost as unpleasant as Nicholas Marsolet. He was glad neither would be at Quebec that winter.

Etienne, who had laughed till his rattles whirred at Savignon's ideas of a French wife's duties, told him that Indian girls made the best moccasins. He danced a few steps in his new ones, clapped Savignon on the back in a friendly way and set off with the Hurons. Champlain had told him to go as far as he could towards the ocean the Indians had told about and to come back next year to the rapids and report what he had found. He gave him paper to make maps and told him to draw on birch bark when that was gone.

Champlain and Tom went back to Quebec. Tom portaged their baggage around the swiftest, highest drop in the rapids but Champlain shot down through the fierce water in a canoe paddled by two Indians. The first white man who had ever tried to shoot the rapids had been drowned. Etienne had been the first white man ever to come down the torrent alive. Champlain was the second to come safely through that treacherous water. On it a canoe was only a floating birch leaf. It might easily vanish when the hurrying water met a hidden wall of rock, leaped high above it, then foamed on.

"The Indians say," Tom had told him, "that you must take off your coat so it will not get wet and hold fast to the crosspieces of the canoe."

So Champlain had come down the rapids of La Chine, sitting quietly in his shirt. Even the strongest swimmers feared these rapids but Champlain had looked calmly downstream as the world of water seemed at once to sink below him and rise around him.

He wrote in his journal: "Even the bravest who have not passed this place in a canoe cannot do so without apprehension."

If he felt it, he did not show it. To these Indians as to many others, he was more than ever Champlain Renowned for Valor.

He shot the rapids on July 17th, 1611. He reached Three Rivers that day and Quebec the next. There were more rose-bushes to set out.

"Water my roses," was the last thing Champlain said as he started on another of his many voyages to France.

Tom climbed to the rock and watched the shallop hurrying downstream with the current, wind and tide. It soon vanished behind the big island where the grapes grew. He walked slowly down to the habitation. The soil around the roses was drying already in the fierce blaze of the July sun. As he watered them, he felt, he thought, as lonely as Savignon going back into a wilderness where no one believed that the French King rolled around in a gold wigwam dragged by eight moose without horns.

CHAPTER 10

GOVERNOR OF CANADA

THE WINTER was long, so it was like every other winter. It was the spring that was different. When the ice went out, there was always the feeling at the habitation that they would see Champlain soon. They knew he would sail from France in March or April and be at Tadoussac six or seven weeks later. Some bright morning the news would come up the river that he was there.

At the habitation men would begin to sweep out the litter of old bones, scattered ashes and wood shavings in which they had been living comfortably all winter. They would polish the high table with beeswax and turpentine, chase Minette off the red cushion of Champlain's chair and brush her white hairs off it, clean guns, sharpen hatchets, load the cannon for a salute, run up the blue and white flag. Sometimes they even washed the floors and pulled weeds out of the cabbages.

Early in April that spring of 1612, Tom began to watch the river but no canoe brought a message to tell them Champlain was at Tadoussac. One day a Basque trader stopped at the habitation on his way to Three Rivers. He found Tom in the garden pruning rosebushes. He said nothing to Tom about his master but from that day on, the habitation was full of rumors.

Tom sturdily refused to believe them and in the daytime he did not. At night however they echoed in his brain as he tried to sleep.

"Champlain is dead, killed when his horse fell on him..." "No, not dead, but he'll never cross the ocean again..." "Anyway he was already out of favor at court... The fur trading company is broken up... Champlain will not be Lieutenant Governor again even if he can walk... The habitation will be pulled down... The traders will meet at Tadoussac..." "No, he was not killed by his horse, he died of a fever..." "Dead or alive he will never come to Quebec again..."

Yet Tom still watched the river, still dug around the roses. Even after the June trading with the Indians was over, he still hoped his master might come. The Indians who shot the rapids that year were angry because Champlain was not there. The Hurons had come to guide him to their far-off country where they lived near a great lake of sweet water. They expected in return that Champlain would help them against their enemies. Tom went to the rapids and explained to the Indians that his master was ill and would come another year.

The Indians must have sensed that Tom was saying only what he hoped, not what he knew. They went off, taking their furs with them. Some said angrily that Champlain had broken his promise to them. Others were sad because the Man of Iron was dead. Savignon, who came to the rapids wearing his French coat and the beaver hat, had told them that a moose without horns had fallen on Champlain and killed him.

There was always some truth in the rumors that went so swiftly through the wilderness. It was true that the reason Champlain did not meet the Indians at the rapids that spring was that his horse had fallen on him and crushed him.

However, he was not dead.

He had lain helpless and close to death for many weeks. The Basque traders, eager to get the fur trade for themselves, had spread the report that Champlain was dead and that the habitation would be pulled down.

As Champlain wrote: "They wanted other men to expose themselves to a thousand dangers, to discover new lands and people, to have all the hardship while they have the profit. It is not reasonable for one man to catch the lamb and another to go off with the wool."

By the time news came from Champlain himself the Basques had carried off most of the furs.

That next winter was worse than the one before. Without Champlain's supervision the food provided for the habitation was not enough for the men there. It was a starving winter for the Montagnais. Their smoked eels did not last long. They killed few moose. By the spring of 1613, they were so hungry that when Pontgravé's ship arrived in the river below Tadoussac they swarmed around it in their canoes, scraping off the tallow with which it was coated with their fingernails and eating it as a great treat.

The latest rumor they had heard was that Champlain was

alive after all, that he was on the ship. They rushed all over it but could find him nowhere.

Champlain liked to play games with his savage friends. He hid in a corner near the cabin, hiding his face in his hands. An old Indian, who had been in the fight at Cape Victory, came up behind him. He saw the scars on Champlain's ear and neck where the arrow had struck him.

"Who is this?" he cried out, seizing Champlain by the ear.

Champlain jumped up and embraced him. The Indian shouted to his friends and they all yelled for joy. The French ships—there were five of them—sailed on to Tadoussac. Tom heard from a half-starved Montagnais who had come to the habitation for beans and bread that the French ships had been seen near Ile Percée. He hurried down to Tadoussac and was there to stand beside his master as Champlain read his new commission from the King.

It said that all trading with the Indians was in the hands of the fur company but that any French trader could join the company by paying fees. Champlain was to live at Quebec, keep it fortified and command the garrison. He was to make all people subject to the King and instruct them in the Catholic religion. He was to explore the St. Lawrence and the seas north of it and find a road to China and the Indies. He was to seek for gold and copper and diamonds.

In his spare time! Tom thought.

He missed another long list of duties but heard that his master had the right to make war and to seize the ships and goods of unlicensed traders.

Some of the Basque traders were standing on the beach

looking glum and defiant. They did not like what they heard. A large group of Montagnais squatted around Champlain listening gravely. After he had finished reading, Tom explained to them in their tongue what his master said.

They understood that Champlain was now in every way the ruler of Canada. They shouted their approval, stamping on the sand and saying *Ho! Ho! Ho!*

The traders scowled and grumbled but finally said that they were loyal subjects of the King and that they would obey Champlain. He gave them temporary licenses to trade.

Pontgravé roared that he would have chased them down the river with his guns. No doubt he would have enjoyed a fight with them. It would not have been the first one. Champlain, however, always preferred peace to war. Trading went on without bloodshed.

Unfortunately there were few furs that year. The Indians were disappointed by not meeting Champlain the year before and discouraged by rumors of his death. Instead of an army of canoes dancing down the rapids, there were only a few scattered parties.

Champlain decided to go up the Ottawa River himself and let the Hurons and Algonquins know that there were many French goods at the rapids, that he was still alive and ready to help them against their enemies. He asked the Indians to give him three canoes and three Indian guides. They gave him only two canoes and one guide, so he could take only four Frenchmen with him.

Tom, who now spoke both Algonquin and Huron well, went as interpreter. Another of the party was Nicholas de Vignau.

Nicholas had appeared suddenly at the French court in the autumn of 1612. One of the Sieur de Monts' secretaries had brought him there. He had an amazing story to tell and he told it well.

He had spent the winter before far up the Ottawa River with Chief Tessouat's tribe. Tessouat was an old one-eyed Algonquin Indian who could still see more with one eye than most white men could with two. Tessouat, according to Nicholas, could still stop a bull moose plunging through snowdrifts with a single arrow. From Tessouat's camp, Nicholas said, he had gone north on snowshoes, traveling under the shooting green glare of northern lights, by starlight, or by moonlight, for the sun made only a small circle above the horizon in those short days of December. It would hang like a dull red lamp for a while above the earth, then go down again among flaming clouds that turned gray all too soon.

He went always north, traveling so fast that he soon reached the great Northern Sea where the ice and snow, looking green in the moonlight, churned in black water.

"Ondathra, my guide, told me that if I had only gone straight from the falls, I could have made the journey in seventeen days," Nicholas said. "But of course," he added modestly, "he could travel faster than I. Still, we made the trip to the sea in a little over a week and were back at Tessouat's cabin a week later."

"The sea, what of the Northern Sea?" Champlain had asked excitedly. "How do you know it was the sea and not an inland lake?"

"In the first place," Nicholas de Vignau said, "it was salt.

In the second, we found the wreck of an English ship. It had sailed there searching for the Northwest Passage to China, would have found it perhaps, if it had not run upon a rock in a storm. The Englishmen got ashore but they were hungry and tried to take food by force from the Indians who lived near by. The Indians were angry and killed the Englishmen. They said there were eighty of them. It may well be true. I saw many scalps hanging in their cabins, some brown-haired, some fair. One they valued much was red."

"There were no survivors?"

"Yes, one. A young English boy. I do not speak English nor he French but we talked a little in Algonquin. He told me his Captain's name—Henry Hudson, I am not sure if I say it right..."

Henry Hudson! The name made de Monts and Champlain shake their heads gravely. They had heard rumors of the death of that brave explorer. So it was true...

"They know about the Sieur de Champlain even in that cold wilderness," young de Vignau went on. "The boy asked me to tell you that the Indians would keep him till you came, sir. I think you could buy him for a few hatchets."

"This is a strange story, Nicholas," Champlain said. "I hope it is true. There will be a great reward for you if it is."

Nicholas de Vignau swore loudly that every word he said was the truth. He even made an oath in the presence of a notary about what he had seen and took the pen in his own fat fist to make his mark. He promised to guide Champlain to where the wrecked ship lay.

It was known in France that the English had lost some ships to the north and there were those rumors of Hudson's death.

The story must be true, Champlain thought, his heart beating a little faster than usual. He saw himself in China, saw all the marvels about which Marco Polo wrote, saw his ship and other French ships coming into Honfleur, laden with spices and with silk robes embroidered with birds and butterflies, with big porcelain jars of candied ginger, with chests of tea lined with scarlet and gold paper.

So Nicholas de Vignau, with the fat white face and the shifting green eyes, with the pouting mouth and the high whining voice that went on and on about killing seals under the northern lights, was chosen by Champlain to go with him up the Ottawa. Tom wished it had been almost anyone else. The idea of hearing that voice for hundreds of miles was one he did not enjoy. He had listened quietly to the story about the journey several times. Nicholas was always ready to tell it and usually remembered new details every time. Once Tom asked him how his guide happened to have a Huron name. Ondathra, which means muskrat, was one of the first Huron words Tom had learned.

Nicholas did not answer for a moment. Then he said, raising his arched eyebrows scornfully above his green eyes, "Why, I suppose because he *was* a Huron. His family were all killed by the Iroquois and Tessouat took him to live in his cabin."

"You learned to speak Huron from him, I hope," Champlain said.

"Why, no, sir. He had learned to speak Algonquin well so we used it."

"He might be useful to us if he can speak both," Champlain said. "What did you say his name was? Ondathra? Remember that, Thomas."

Tom did remember it.

They left the Ile de Ste. Hélène on May 27th. By the twenty-ninth they had passed the great rapids of La Chine, partly by land, carrying canoes, food and arms, partly by paddling against the swift, endless flow of the river. They traveled by day and at night barricaded themselves and took turns keeping watch.

"The Iroquois," Champlain warned, "would give us as good a welcome as they would the Hurons if they found us."

No Iroquois found them. Their difficulties were in passing the many falls and rapids that were between them and Chief Tessouat's island. Sometimes they portaged, sometimes they paddled up the rapids.

"This," Champlain noted, "makes one sweat."

He observed with pleasure the skill the Indians showed, winding past eddies of white surf, choosing the easiest places at a glance. He listened to the frightful noise of the river, which in some places foamed so white as it fell that no water could be seen. Often the woods were so thick that, to get the canoe up the rapids, they dragged it along by a rope, keeping on the edge of the stream.

"In drawing mine," Champlain wrote later, "I nearly lost my life. It crossed an eddy and if it had not by good fortune caught between two rocks, it would have dragged me in. I could not undo the rope quickly enough. It was around my hand and nearly cut it off.

"In this danger I cried to God and began to pull on my canoe which came to me again by the backward flow of the water, which occurs in these falls. I thanked God and begged him to preserve us. My savage came to help me but I was out of danger. It was necessary to save the canoe at all costs because without it I would have had to wait until some Indians came that way, a poor hope for those who have nothing to dine on. Our Frenchmen had no better luck than I, being several times near death, but God preserved us all. We rested the remainder of the day, having done enough."

They thought they must have passed the worst falls but an Indian, one of a party they met, told them they had seen nothing yet. From this party Champlain got another guide. He sent one of his Frenchmen back to Quebec with a report of his journey written on a leaf torn from his notebook.

Waterfall after waterfall stood in the way. Where one river flowed into the Ottawa, there was a fall forty-five feet high. The water fell with such force that it made a curtain, springing from the wall of rock, four hundred feet broad. His guides showed Champlain how to walk under it without getting wet except from the fine steam thrown off by the tumbling water.

Champlain called this fall—and the river from which it came—the Rideau, which means the Curtain. At another fall, as high as the Curtain and almost a mile wide, the water had hollowed out a deep basin in which foam boiled furiously with a circular motion. The Indians called this fall the *Asticou*, which means kettle or boiler. Champlain called it the Chaudière, which means the same thing. They could hear the noise of the Chaudière five miles away. Even Nicholas de Vignau's high voice was silenced by that roar.

Farther up the river the water came down sixty feet in a gradual slope, making a marvellous noise.

"What do they call this one?" Champlain asked Tom.

"They say it is called Racoon Rapids, sir. You know, what we call Chats Sauvages, the animals with rings on their tails and black masks on their faces."

"I will call it Rapides des Chats," Champlain said.

He stopped long enough to add it to the maps that he was always drawing in his notebook and to figure out the latitude of the place with his astrolabe.

To pass these rapids they left behind them most of their load, including their clothes and their cornmeal. They kept only their weapons and their fish lines. With the canoes lightened, they succeeded in paddling up the rapids, then went back by land and brought the things they left behind. Champlain admired the way the Indians endured these hardships and the perfect balance that made it possible for them to stand up in canoes and paddle against the current, avoiding rocks and eddies.

On one of the islands they made a cross of red cypress. Tom carved the arms of France on it and they set it up on a high place. They paddled up a small fall the next day. At the top of it, the Indians took the sacks of provisions out of the canoes and hid them in the woods. They told Tom that they must now go a long distance overland. In that way they would avoid several difficult falls.

This decision caused a dispute between the Indians and Nicholas. He said to them and to Champlain that there was no danger, that they ought to go by water.

The Indians burst out into angry speech.

"What is it? What are they saying?" Champlain asked Tom.

Tom said, "One of them said to Nicholas 'You are tired of living?' And the others told me to tell you that you must not believe him, he lies."

"I had several times observed," Champlain wrote that evening, "that Nicholas had little knowledge of the river so I followed the advice of the Indians and went by land. I was loaded with only three arquebuses, three paddles, my clock and small articles. My men carried more. Our chief trouble was mosquitoes. After six or seven miles, we were so weary we could go no farther, having eaten nothing but a little broiled fish for twenty-four hours. On the edge of a pond we made a fire to drive away the mosquitoes and caught more fish. The perseverance of the mosquitoes is so marvellous I cannot describe it."

The next day was the worst yet. A windstorm had blown down huge pines on top of each other. The travelers had to crawl over or under them. At last they reached a lake—Muskrat Lake they called it—where there was good fishing. Here Champlain lost his astrolabe. He was quite sure he had had it when they made their camp but the next morning it was not to be found. Tom always thought that Nicholas knew where it was though Nicholas firmly denied having seen it for two days.

"Well, it's one thing less to carry," Champlain said cheerfully. "I may have dropped it crawling under those pines."

His maps became less accurate from this time. The extraordinary thing was that he could make any maps at all of the twisting rivers and trails.   Beyond Muskrat Lake, they found a settlement where Indians had planted gardens and grew corn.

"Nibachis, their chief, visited us," Champlain wrote. "He was much astonished that we could have passed the falls and the bad roads. He offered us tobacco then said to his companions that we must have fallen from the clouds. Now, he said, he believed what other Indians had said of me. Through Thomas, our interpreter, I said that I had pleasure in meeting them and that I had come to help them in their wars, that I would like to go farther and see other chiefs. They promised to help me. They showed me their gardens. The corn was four fingers high."

Nibachis guided Champlain, as he had promised, to Chief Tessouat's island which lay in a widening of the Ottawa River.

Tessouat could not believe that he was really looking at Champlain.

"It is like a dream," he said. "You must rest now," he added. "Tomorrow we will hold a great feast in your honor."

CHAPTER 11

PASSAGE TO CHINA

THE *TABAGIE* would be like other feasts, Champlain supposed. He would be half choked with tobacco, which he had never learned to like. His legs would be stiff from sitting on the ground and his ears deafened by Indian singing and the stamp of dancing feet. There would be *sagamité*, that repulsive porridge with fish scales and bones and leathery meat in it. There would be endless speeches which Thomas would have to translate to him. Then he would have to make a speech in return. Luckily Thomas spoke crisply and cleanly, with the proper pauses for courtesy. Nicholas was of little use. He would rush at a sentence in his high, whining voice and then stop in the middle of it, fumbling for a word. Still, if he led them to the Passage to China, much might be overlooked.

The *tabagie* would take much time, a whole day probably, and Champlain wanted to be on his way towards the Northern Sea. However, he knew that if he was to get guides and canoes from the Indians he must be patient.

After all, he thought, it could not be more tiresome than

standing around at the French court, watching the courtiers bowing and jigging their way through some new dance while fiddles scraped and oboes sighed. He yawned as he thought of the weary afternoons he had spent waiting for some minister to remember to write out the commission that made Champlain the ruler of Canada.

Before long he would have to go back to Paris and report on the fur trade. That was always first in people's minds in France. They would agree with him, as they had politely a hundred times, that missionaries must be sent to Canada to make Christians of what they liked to call the Noble Savages. Champlain knew well that no missionaries would be sent unless he continued to visit France and talk about the Indians. If he could return with news of the Northwest Passage to China, that would stir things up.

Tom walked around the island with his master early that morning. They saw the place where the Indians buried their dead. The graves were marked with large pieces of wood with a figure of a man or a woman carved on them. A man would have a shield, a spear, a bow and arrows. A chief would have feathers on his head and *matachias*, as the Indians called ornaments of beads and porcupine quills. For a woman there would be a kettle and a wooden spoon, perhaps a paddle. Sometimes instead of carving, there was painting, neatly done in red and yellow.

"They tell me," Tom said, "that when they bury a warrior, they put his best beaver robe with him and his other treasures—hatchets, kettles, knives—so that these things will help him where he is going."

"They believe in life after death, then?" Champlain asked.

"Yes," Tom said. "They believe everything has a soul—dogs, beavers, even women, even kettles. A man who had lost a kettle told me that his kettle was dead but its soul had gone wherever the souls of kettles go."

They walked through the gardens where squash vines were in flower.

"Why do they live on this island where the soil is so poor and sandy? It reminds me of St. Croix," Champlain said with a shudder.

"They say that because of the rapids the Iroquois cannot reach them here. That may be one reason, but our guide told me that it is because they control the traffic of the river. No one can pass without making them a present. When the Hurons come down with their furs and when they go back with their French goods, they are stopped at the portage by one of Tessouat's men. He says sadly that Tessouat has lost an uncle or a dear cousin—he had as many cousins as a crow—and that to cure his grief he needs a present. And next year it is the same thing."

Champlain laughed. "And some people think the Indians are not civilized," he said. "Why, we might be in Paris! Well, luckily I have some knives and strings of beads left."

The guests now began to come to Tessouat's cabin for the *tabagie*. They were the handsomest, cleanest Indians Champlain had seen. They were neatly painted in elaborate designs. Their deerskin robes were beautifully ornamented with beads and quills. Much time had been spent in arranging their hair. Some had long hair on one side and the rest of the scalp shaved.

Some had kept only a single lock. Others had braids bound with *matachias*. Each man brought his porringer and wooden spoon. There was meat roasting on the coals. Champlain was glad to have some instead of *sagamité*. The drink was fine clear water such as one could not get in Paris.

The guests all sat on the ground and Chief Tessouat served them. He ate nothing himself. The Indians considered it rude to eat before the guests had satisfied their hunger.

"When the *tabagie* was over," Champlain wrote, "the young men who had been sitting near the door of the cabin withdrew. All who stayed filled their pipes. We smoked half an hour in silence, as is their custom. Then I explained to them, through Thomas, my interpreter, that I came to assure them of my friendship and to help them against their enemies, as I had done before. I had many men at the rapids for whom a messenger could be sent. I said I wished to see their country, their lakes and rivers, especially the Northern Sea. I asked them to lend me four canoes and men to guide me to the Nipissings. There I would get guides to the sea."

The Indians smoked again and spoke together in low tones. Then Tessouat, speaking for all said, "You have been a better friend to us than any Frenchman. We feel as kindly to you as to our children. But last year you did not come to meet us at the Great Rapids. Two thousand warriors went to meet you ready for war. The French told us you were dead. We believed it. They would not help us in war. Some treated our men badly. We decided not to return to the rapids this year but to go to war without you. Twelve hundred men have gone. We will give you canoes, but unwillingly, for the Nipissings whom you wish to visit are bad people, sorcerers. They have killed some of our people with magic herbs. Also the roads are dangerous."

Champlain said that the roads could not be worse than those by which he had come. As to the herbs, he would not eat them. So, after consulting together, they promised to lend him the canoes.

He left them and walked through the gardens. He saw French peas in flower. He was happy because he was looking at French plants so far away in the wilderness and because he would soon be on the road to the Northwest Passage.

Thomas stayed behind in the smoky cabin. Scraps of talk he had heard made him sure that the Indians had not spoken frankly to Champlain. After talking together a little while, they told him to tell his master that after all they could not give him the canoes. All the Frenchmen would die on such a journey. No one was willing to go as a guide. Tom had better tell his master to wait until next year. Then they would send a large party of warriors to protect him from the Nipissings.

Tom carried the message to Champlain, who went back to the cabin with him. Nicholas de Vignau still sat smoking by the door.

"I said," Champlain wrote, "that I was sorry they showed me so little friendship. I pointed to Nicholas and said that he had been to the Nipissing country and had not found the roads so bad.

"Then they all stared at Nicholas and Tessouat, the old chief, calling him by name, said: 'Nicholas, is it true that you said you were among the Nipissings?'

"He hesitated long, looking at the smoke of his pipe, then said in their tongue: 'Yes, I was there.'

"They then threw themselves on him, as if they would eat him or tear him to pieces, uttering loud cries.

"Tessouat said to him: 'You are a downright liar! You know well that you slept at my side every night, with my children, that winter you stayed here, and arose every morning. If you were among the Nipissings, it was while you slept! How could you lead your chief to believe lies and expose his life to so many dangers? You are a rogue and should be put to death. Now I see it is because of your lies that he spoke of the little friend-ship we showed him.'"

They went outside the cabin. Champlain spoke to Nicholas, who hung his head: "Speak the truth, Nicholas. If you have really been to the sea, I will reward you, but you must cause me no more trouble."

"I'll guide you there if they'll give us a canoe," Nicholas said.

Champlain had Thomas tell this to Tessouat.

"You do wrong to trust a liar who would cause your death instead of brave chiefs who are your friends," Tessouat said.

Champlain then had Tom tell them the whole story as he had heard it from Nicholas—the wrecked vessel on the coast of the Northern Sea, the fair-haired scalps, the English boy waiting to be ransomed with French hatchets. The Indians cried out louder than ever, calling Nicholas a liar. They asked him who his guide was and by what lakes and rivers he had gone. He replied that he had forgotten the name of the guide.

"Though," Champlain wrote, "he had told it to me twenty times and even the day before."

Champlain brought out a map of the country Nicholas had drawn. The Indians questioned him about it but he kept a sullen silence.

At last, in the presence of the Frenchmen, Champlain told him that further pretending was out of the question. Nicholas must say if he had seen these things or not.

"If I go farther in vain," Champlain said, "I will have you hanged. That will be your only reward."

At last Nicholas fell on his knees asking Champlain's pardon. He confessed that all he had said, both in France and in Canada, was false. He had never seen the sea, never had been farther than Tessouat's village.

"I only said it so I could return to Canada," he whispered.

Champlain had him removed. For once his patience was exhausted.

"I could endure the sight of him no longer," he wrote. "I had Thomas ask him for details. Nicholas said he thought I would never undertake the journey because of the dangers. Or that something would prevent it such as the Indians not giving us canoes. He said if we would leave him with Tessouat, he would go on until he found the sea or died. I was not impressed by this offer, only astounded by his malice and boldness. I see now that my guides were right when they told me that he counted on my drowning in some of the rapids we passed. He told Thomas he hoped to get a reward in France for his discovery."

The Indians, hearing that he had confessed, said he ought to be put to death. Tessouat added: "Do you not see that he meant to cause your death? Give him to us. We promise you that he will not lie any more."

They ran towards Nicholas, their children all running and yelling and shouting.

Champlain raised his hand. They stopped.

"Do not harm him," he said. "I will take him to the great rapids and show him to the gentlemen there, to whom he promised to bring salt water. They will do him justice."

As he spoke for his master, Tom had never admired him so much. Champlain was shorter than the shortest of the chiefs of La Chine. He never raised his voice or changed his courteous manner. Yet his courage was so great that the yelling mob respected his raised hand. His sense of justice was so keen that he would not take personal vengeance on this liar and traitor who might well have caused his death.

Champlain decided to return to the La Chine rapids. He told the Indians that there were four ships there loaded with French goods and he asked them to go with him. So they set out, forty canoes speeding down the Ottawa, leaving that Northern Sea, as Champlain said, "only in my imagination." They met other canoes on the way. The news that Champlain was alive and in Canada had spread through the wilderness. Before long there were sixty canoes in their party and they overtook twenty more, heavily loaded with furs.

Between Tessouat's island and the place where they had left the river to go by land, they passed six bad falls. Champlain saw clearly why his guides had advised him to make the long portage and why Nicholas had so boldly said that the river was not dangerous.

When they came to the Chaudière, boiling loudly in its foaming basin, they carried their canoes around the fall. There was a rock that looked like the head of a giant with his mouth open near the fall. As they reached a point near the rock they stopped and handed around a wooden plate. Everyone put a bit of tobacco into it. Then they gathered around the plate, dancing and singing. One of the chiefs made a speech saying that this offering to the guardian spirit of the fall would protect them against evil spirits on their journey. He then took the plate and tossed the tobacco into the Chaudière while all the Indians shouted. Though their voices were loud, the roaring of the fall was still louder. They could hear it far behind them as they traveled on downstream.

"These poor people," Champlain wrote in his notebook, "think they cannot make a safe journey without this ceremony. Their enemies often wait for them at this portage and surprise them there. They are safe from the Iroquois above the Chaudière. They go no farther because of the difficulty of the journey."

When they reached the great rapids of La Chine on June 17th, 1613, the barges there saluted them with their cannon. This delighted their friends, astonishing those who had never heard such music. Afterwards Champlain called the French together and made Nicholas confess publicly what he had done. He then pardoned him, telling him that he would allow him to stay in Canada, as he asked, and search for the Northwest Passage.

However, no Indian would take this liar with him. Champlain never heard of him again.

CHAPTER 12

IROQUOIS FORT

AFTER THE trading was over Tom said goodbye to his master. He did not see him again for nearly two years. The task Champlain had given him was to go with the Hurons into their country, to learn to speak the language well and to explore as far west as he could. He was to make maps and notes of all he found. He was also to persuade the Hurons to bring their furs to the foot of the La Chine rapids every year, whether they heard Champlain was there or not.

Champlain hoped, when he came back, to bring missionaries with him. The last words that Thomas heard him say were: "May God by his grace bring to his honor and glory the conversion of these poor savages!"

To some of his most loyal friends among the Indian chiefs Champlain had given the title of Captain. It was with Captain Darontal that Tom Lee spent the winter of 1614 and 1615. He did all that Champlain asked him, exploring the Great Lakes that are drained by the St. Lawrence River, making maps of them, learning the difficult Huron language until he could think in it.

The Hurons became fond of him. Even the medicine men, who had looked suspiciously at Tom's surgical tools at first, used to call him in when there were bad wounds to sew up or broken legs to be set. One of them even learned to help Tom although, to be on the safe side, he always began by talking to his magic stone. It was a black stone with two reddish stripes running around it. Very powerful, the owner said. He told Tom that if he found its brother, he would give it to him for one of his sharp knives.

Tom said politely that he feared he would never learn to say the right words to a stone. He offered to teach the medicine man how to sew up a wound. The Huron, who was interested in the knife as a weapon, declined the offer with many courteous expressions and the two doctors remained good friends. Each had his own special work and admired the other's skill. The medicine man said that much illness was in the mind, that he cured the mind and the body healed itself. However, when he broke his arm he was glad to have Tom set it.

They lived in the same long house and shared the same fire. There were two families to every fire. The Huron houses were very different from any of the Indian cabins Tom had seen before. Each side was made by driving rows of saplings six feet apart into the earth. Their tops were bent towards the center of the building and lashed together. The outside was covered with slabs of bark except for a narrow opening along the length of the roof. This let in a little light and let out parts of the smoke from the cooking fires.

Inside between the saplings there was a double row of bunks. The lower ones were used as beds and the upper ones were usually filled with possessions—furs, kettles, weapons. Strings of dried corn hung from the roof to keep them away from the mice.

There were fewer mice in the house where Tom lived than in the others because he had brought Minette with him. He could not bear to leave her behind in Quebec. She was a large and stately cat now. She spent most of her time lying on Tom's old blue camlet cloak. A good deal of her white fur came off on it, giving it a frosted look, much admired by the medicine man's daughters. Minette did not catch many mice but she frightened some away. Tom wished she would frighten the fleas as well but that was too much to expect. Where there were Indians there would be fleas.

Soon after Minette arrived, she had four kittens—two fluffy tiger kittens, a white one with a black nose and one yellow one. She taught them to wash their faces and catch mice. They learned themselves how to chase their tails and fluff up and spit at the Indian dogs. They clawed their way to the upper bunks when the dogs chased them and added hair of various colors to the camlet cloak. The Indians loved them. They thought the tiger-striped ones were a kind of racoon. They called the white one Snow Man and the yellow one Sunflower.

Even without the kittens there was always plenty going on in the long house. Tom would come in from the porch, where food was stored, and look into the smoky darkness. At first he would see nothing except the glowing fires, ten of them spaced a dozen feet apart down the long passage. It would be so smoky and noisy that at first he could neither see nor hear what was happening. Then he would begin to see women bending over kettles. Every family had at least one iron kettle now. Around them raced the children, chasing the dogs who were chasing the cats. The dogs did not bark but they made a low growling sound. The children had turtle shells with stones in them which they rattled and little skin drums full of grains of corn which they shook. They all yelled, of course.

The papoose boards with the papooses strapped to them would be leaning up against the bunks. The fire would shine on the babies' black eyes as they watched the leaps and bounds of their brothers and sisters.

Farther down the house, a dance might be going on because someone was ill. The patient's bunk would be heaped with presents in case longing for a kettle or a string of beads was causing the illness. The medicine man would jump around, shouting and grabbing hot coals out of the fire, stopping occasionally to talk to his magic stone. Then he would bite the patient's neck and show everyone a small sharp stone like an arrowhead that he had pulled out of the flesh with his teeth. With the stone came the bad spirit, he said, that was making her ill.

Tom saw these stones many times. They were so strangely alike that he came to the conclusion that it was always the same stone and that the medicine man had it in his mouth all the time. Even if he did, it seemed to work because the sick girl—it was usually a girl—often got up soon and danced with the others.

Around another fire Darontal and his chiefs might be smoking and holding counsel. Outside, young men with netted sticks in their hands would be whirling a ball from one net to another. Tom became quite skillful at this game, which the Frenchmen called lacrosse. Naturally the tall Indians with their long arms had an advantage over him but he was quicker on his feet than many of them and accurate at catching the ball. When they went to play against another village they used to take him along.

They would walk twenty miles through the woods for a game, taking furs and axes with them to stake on their skill. All the young men in both villages would play. They would hang their furs and other treasures on the goals, which might be a mile apart, and play all day. The side that won the game won everything on the goal.

More than once the players from Captain Darontal's village tramped home barefoot in the dark, having lost not only their furs and hatchets but their moccasins too. No one ever complained even when he had a broken collarbone or ribs. Tom often set broken legs and, after the game was over, helped to carry the patient home. No matter what happened, they came home as cheerfully as they started.

Once they carried their canoes several miles to a lake and paddled to a village at the upper end of it. The lacrosse ball was soon being scooped from one net to another. Tom was dodging through a crowd of players near the other goal, hoping to catch the ball and shoot it in. Two tall players from the other village crashed into them.

"Excuse me, gosling," said a voice above him.

"Your pardon, sir," said another.

Tom looked up. Etienne and Savignon were looking down at him, laughing.

"Certainly," Tom said politely, caught the ball, and sent it whizzing into the goal.

There was a *tabagie* for the players after the game was over. Tom sat on the ground between Etienne and Savignon. Only they did not call him Savignon any more. He was known as Paris-France because that was all he ever talked about.

He began at once.

Did Tom remember a great torchlight procession when the windows of all the dark houses shone red and some of them caught fire? How the flames rose up like a mountain and roared like the Chaudière? Did he remember how they went to the King's palace and saw him at dinner with a golden canoe full of salt in front of him? He was eating roast goose cooked in wine. How neatly he ate with his knife and his golden spoon! Did Tom remember that the King once threw a snowball at him, Savignon? Did he remember the tennis court where the King hit a ball around with a small snowshoe? No, Tom was right—not a shoe, a racket...

Indians around them had stopped talking and were listening to Savignon.

"Do you remember," Savignon went on, "how we saw the King in his rolling cabin of gold, pulled by eight moose without horns?"

At this—they had been waiting for it—the Indians all burst out laughing. It was evidently their favorite joke. Poor Savignon! To have seen wonders, never to be believed—it was hard.

Darontal's village won the lacrosse game that day and went home loaded with furs and *matachias*. Tom was given a handsome belt decorated with red and yellow porcupine quills. He wore it when they started for the great rapids of La Chine.

The Indians had been disappointed not to find Champlain at

the rapids in 1614 but Tom had persuaded the men of Darontal's village and of the villages nearby to take their furs again this year. Etienne brought many canoes from the villages in his part of the country. Paris-France was there in his beaver hat. It was looped up now with an ornament of an eagle's feather, porcupine quills and a carefully stuffed hummingbird. Savignon had made it himself.

They traveled many miles a day. As more canoes joined them, the camps at night became bigger and busier. More men were cutting saplings for shelters, lopping off balsam boughs for beds, spinning sticks to make fire. More squaws were bringing in dry wood and setting trout to sizzle over the fire. This was the only meal of the day. When they caught no fish, they ate a little parched corn made into thin *sagamité*.

On the way up the river the year before, when they lightened their loads, they had buried corn wrapped in birch bark near the trails. Now they would find it again and use it. Paris-France had much to say—and none of it flattering—about Indian cooking. For one thing he objected to there being ashes and twigs and insects in the *sagamité*.

"It was not like that in the Street of the Bear," he said.

Etienne, however, ate whatever was in the *sagamité* and liked it. He said that grasshoppers made it very nourishing. Paris-France only groaned and wished he had some goose liver pâté with truffles.

"There'll be a feast tonight at La Chine," Tom told him, but they both knew there would be no truffles in it.

On May 25th, 1615, they shot the great rapids and made their camp on the Island of Montreal. There were Basque traders already near the island ready to do business. Champlain had not arrived and the traders said he was not coming this year so trading had better start. Tom, who had been talking to some Montagnais Indians, called to Darontal to keep his beavers.

"The Sieur de Champlain is on his way," he shouted, and the whole camp yelled for joy and began dancing.

Soon a messenger came from Champlain, a figure as strange to the Indians as a Man of Iron, though familiar to Tom from his school days. It was Father Joseph Le Caron, a Franciscan priest of the Recollet order. At last Champlain had persuaded Christian missionaries to come to Canada and here was the first one, in his long robe of grayish wool and his heavy wooden sandals, ready to face the dangers of the Canadian wilderness. He was so eager to begin his work of bringing Christianity to the Indians that he had not even stopped at Quebec but had traveled as fast as a canoe would take him to Montreal.

He would spend the winter with the Hurons and learn their language, he told Tom, who acted as his interpreter, but first he must return to Quebec and get his church ornaments and other things he needed. Tom and Etienne gladly paddled him down to Quebec.

Champlain was there with three other priests. He was having lodgings and a chapel built for them. The habitation was humming with activity. Of course it was out of repair. It always was unless Champlain was there. Now men were patching roofs, sawing boards, planting seeds. They were, Tom noticed, even sweeping out the Great Hall and brushing the hair of one of Minette's daughters, now the head of the cat colony, off the cushions of the governor's chair. Someone had actually polished the pewter and the youngest boy was melting up broken spoons in one of the cook's ladles and making new ones.

Barrels of biscuit and casks of wine were being rolled into the storehouse. The smith was pounding out new hinges and making the anvil ring. The mason was tucking new mortar with his trowel between loose bricks. Hammers went tack-tack-tack on the heads of nails. No doubt, the Sieur de Champlain was in Quebec.

Father Le Caron wished to return to Montreal at once so that he could be sure of leaving with the Hurons for their country. Champlain gave him many sensible reasons for not spending his first Canadian winter in the wilderness. The priest listened courteously but his zeal was too great.

Then he said, "I wish to learn the character of the people and their tongue. With cheerfulness and God's help, I hope to overcome the difficulties. Little is needed by a man who has vowed himself to perpetual poverty and who seeks only the glory of God. For that I can endure all the sufferings and hardships that may come."

Champlain did not try to keep him from going. He went with him to the rapids. There he met the Hurons and Algonquins. They told him that the Iroquois were bolder than ever. They robbed canoes of furs as they went down the river, stole French goods on the way back, tortured and killed the carriers. Captain Darontal and Captain Iroquet wanted Champlain's help in war against these thieves.

Champlain and Pontgravé decided that it was necessary to punish the Iroquois. With them threatening death at every portage, there could be no trade, no explorations towards the

Pacific, no carrying of Christianity to their friends. Champlain agreed to go to war.

He started back for Quebec. At the Rivière des Prairies he found a great crowd gathered on the shore of the river—Indians in their war paint, French traders, sailors, locksmiths, carpenters and the four priests. It was June 24th, the feast of St. John the Baptist, and the priests said mass while the Indians stood in silent wonder at the chanting, the vestments, the incense and the shining church ornaments.

Two days later Champlain heard the first mass ever said in Quebec. Soon afterwards, twelve French soldiers with Indian guides started up the river with Father Le Caron. Champlain followed with Etienne and Thomas and a party of Indians. Their canoes were low in the water with French goods.

Champlain, Thomas and Etienne knew the way to Chief Tessouat's island now and they reached it safely. They made generous presents to the chief, whose one eye wept for the loss of a dear uncle. Etienne figured that any uncle of Tessouat's would be about a hundred and ten years old. They left him somewhat consoled by their gifts and traveled on up the Ottawa, portaging around many falls. They made three trips at each portage, one for the canoe, two more for its load. When the Indians dragged the canoes along the edge of the river, as they did when there was no good trail alongshore, they were often up to their necks in water.

On July 26th they reached the lake of Nipissings. Those sorcerers, who were supposed to kill their guests with magic herbs, received them kindly and entertained them at a great *tabagie.* Near Lake Huron they found gardens where squashes were ripening and where sunflowers were turning their brown and gold faces towards the sun. They had few provisions left by this time. Early in the journey the Indians had stuffed themselves with all they could eat. This was their custom. The French idea of saving seemed foolish to them.

"You want us to save it for the Iroquois? They are no doubt waiting at the next portage," they said when Tom tried to explain Champlain's ideas about rationing to them.

It was no use. When the food was all gone they ate wild strawberries and blueberries. While they were hunting for blueberries, they met three hundred fierce-looking, naked, tattooed men. Their faces were painted. Beads hung from their ears and nostrils. Their carefully oiled hair was arranged so high on their heads that Champlain gave them the name of Cheveux Relevés (High Hairs).

"They make a fine appearance," he said to Tom. "Their hair is better dressed than the French could do it with curling tongs."

These fierce-looking warriors were picking blueberries. They told Tom that they dried them for use in winter. Champlain gave their chief a hatchet, with which he was delighted. He showed the French how his tribe armed themselves for war with clubs, bows and arrows and shields of buffalo hide.

Lake Huron—Champlain called it the Mer Douce—was full of enormous pike and sturgeon. They spent some time fishing and then paddled along the coast while Champlain filled his notebook with maps of bays, islands and peninsulas. At last they came to Carhagouha, a village with a triple palisade thirty-five feet high around it. Here they found Father Le Caron, who was much surprised to see them. He told them that the Indians had been patient with him though his long robe annoyed them. He had learned to wear it tucked up above his knees so it would not bring mud and water into the canoes. He had not learned much of the language, he said. It was a dreadful language, all grunts. There seemed to be no letter M in it. The nearest they could come to the name of the Blessed Virgin was Ouarie.

Tom helped Father Le Caron learn some of the common words he needed to know. The Indians evidently liked the priest. They had built him a house of saplings covered with bark for a chapel. There, on August 12th, he said the first mass in Ontario. Champlain, the French soldiers and some Indian chiefs were in the little chapel. Tom and Etienne with the Indian guides, visiting Cheveux Relevés, squaws, papooses, small children, and painted warriors knelt outside. The Indians watched the French and carefully copied their motions.

It was a happy day for Champlain. He felt sure that if the trade routes could be kept open, Christianity would travel along with them. As they left the village, he talked with Etienne about his other great desire—to find a passage to the Pacific. Since being deceived by Nicholas de Vignau, he had given up the idea of the far northern route. He had always hoped to find one in a temperate climate. Now, as he looked westward out across Lake Huron and listened to Etienne's description of other lakes still larger, of a vast river he had heard of that might run all the way to China, he began to feel sure that before long Frenchmen would be reaching China that way.

Tom wished he had such stories as Etienne's to tell. He too had heard of the big river that looped for thousands of miles like a great brown snake, the Mississippi, the Indians called it but he had never had guides who would take him as far west as Etienne had gone. The maps he had drawn for his master were accurate and careful as far as they went but Etienne's went much farther. They made the Pacific seem only a few days away.

However, they could not make that journey now. They must go to Cahiagué where plans were being made to punish the Iroquois. There were said to be more than two thousand warriors gathered there. Champlain was disappointed to find only five hundred. Captain Darontal suggested sending to ask their friends the Carantouans to join them. They lived only a few days' journey away, south of the Iroquois country. They could easily send four hundred fighting men, though it would be dangerous to cross Iroquois country. Who would go?

Among the volunteers was Etienne Brulé.

Champlain allowed him to go because he now spoke Huron well. He could report on a new part of the country. Perhaps, he said, he would find the Mississippi. Etienne went off, singing, with twelve Huron braves to cross the Iroquois country and to see what was beyond. The Indians sang too, a Huron war song, and kept time with their paddles. Etienne still wore his belt of rattlesnake skin, Tom noticed, but the rattles were gone from around his neck. Instead he wore a holy medal, an Agnus Dei, that Father Le Caron had given him.

Cahiagué was a town of two hundred houses, some of them more than eighty feet long. There was great feasting and singing and dancing there. Champlain would have started at once for the Iroquois fortress they planned to attack, but though the Indians agreed that it would be a good idea to surprise the

Iroquois they were in no hurry. Champlain knew that they never obeyed any orders that did not please them. He could not command them, only persuade them.

He explained patiently how important it was to act quickly and all together so that the arquebuses could do their best work. The Indians listened with their usual grave politeness and went back to their dancing. Besides eating, dancing and smoking they slept a good deal. There was also hunting and fishing to be done.

Champlain had hoped to start in early August. It was September 5th before the warriors had collected their cornmeal and their weapons and were ready to leave. On the tenth the ground was white with frost. The leaves were changing color all through the forests. They went south in sparkling blue and gold weather, hot at noon with kingfishers flashing blue over shining water, cold at night under bright stars, colder still in the morning mists.

Champlain used his new astrolabe and wrote down the latitude of new lakes and islands. He drew maps showing rivers and their rapids and made notes about the country.

"We passed through," he wrote, "a pleasant region of cleared land. The trees seem to be set out. Grapes were ripe but they had left a tart taste in our mouths. With better cultivation they might make good wine.

"On October 9th our savages took eleven Iroquois prisoners, four women, three boys, a girl, three men. They were going fishing. Captain Iroquet began work by cutting off the finger of one of these poor women. I told him that it was not the act of a warrior, as he called himself, to be cruel to women, who have no defense but their tears. One should treat them kindly on account of their helplessness. I said that what he had done was base and brutal and if repeated would not give me heart to help them in their war."

"Tell your master," Captain Iroquet said to Tom, "that it is the way our enemies treat us. Still, since it displeases him I will not do it to the women. However, I will to the men."

On October 10th they arrived at the Iroquois fort. Champlain's plan was to hide until the next day, reconnoiter the fort and make a surprise attack on it. The Indians would not wait. They wanted to hear the thunder tubes speak. They dashed forward at once to attack the enemy and were soon calling for help.

"I approached the enemy," Champlain wrote, "and though I had but few men, yet we showed them what they had never seen before. As soon as they saw us and heard the arquebus shots and the balls whizzing in their ears, they withdrew speedily to the fort, carrying their dead and wounded. We also had five wounded of whom one died. We withdrew to the main body of our fighters who at once retreated, going too far from the fort.

"I urged them to go on with the fight, using rough and angry words. I knew that if things went according to their whim, utter ruin would result."

With Tom's help he explained to them what they must do. The fort was surrounded by four good palisades made of big pieces of wood lashed together six inches apart. The palisades were thirty feet high, with galleries inside from which the Iroquois could stand and shoot their arrows. The fort was well supplied with water from a pond. There were gutters and

spouts along the galleries so that water could easily be poured on any fire started by the Hurons.

Champlain told them they must build what he called a cavalier. He had drawn a picture of it—a wooden tower higher than the palisades with a platform on top. Four men with arquebuses could stand there. The Indians, he said, must make large wooden shields to protect his men from arrows and others to protect the Indians while they were setting fires. The shields would also keep water away from the fires until they were burning well.

The Indians began work on the cavalier the next morning and finished it in four hours. It took two hundred of their strongest men to carry it. They put it down six feet from the palisade. Three French soldiers climbed it, carrying their arquebuses.

As soon as they began firing, the Iroquois left their galleries. This was the moment to set fires and Champlain ordered the Indians to do so under cover of their wooden shields. They were too excited to obey orders. They only screeched insults and shot arrows into the fort where they did little damage. They set some fires but on the wrong side, in the face of the wind. They had not collected enough dry wood and did not even use what they had.

Champlain soon saw that he could do nothing with this screaming crowd. He decided to do what he could with his own men but they were too few to take the fort. Arrows fell like hail. The men on the cavalier killed and wounded many Iroquois but two Huron chiefs and fifteen other warriors were wounded too. Champlain himself was wounded twice by arrows in his leg and in his knee.

"These wounds," he wrote, "caused me great inconvenience."

The Hurons, as soon as they saw that Champlain and the chiefs were wounded, ran off in disorder. Nothing Champlain could say would make them attack again. He shouted and shouted but they did not listen.

Suddenly he knew why. His servant Thomas was missing.

If the Carantouans would only come, Champlain thought, they might still have a chance, but the Carantouans did not come. The chiefs listened to his stumbling words and they waited, but not long enough. While they were waiting, they had baskets made to carry the wounded. Champlain was trussed up in one of these baskets and the Hurons started back for their village.

"I was so bound that I could move no more than a papoose on its board," Champlain wrote. "I could not stand because of the wound in my knee. I have never suffered such torture, the wound being nothing to being bound to the back of a savage. The enemy followed us for a mile, trying to capture some of the rearguard, but at last gave up and went back.

"The only good point of their warfare is that they retreat safely, placing the wounded in the center, being well armed on the wings and the rear and continuing this order till they reach a safe place. We had to go more than fifty miles before we reached the place on Lake Ontario where we had hidden our canoes. This was hard for the wounded as well as for those who carried us, though the men took turns as carriers. At last we reached the canoes and I could get out of my prison."

He tried, as he was jolted painfully along in his basket, to remember when he had last seen Tom. He never slept but he seemed to dream and, in the dream, pictures of his interpreter floated through his mind. The pictures always included a flash of sunshine on yellow hair. He had seen that flash many times during the battle. He had seen Tom helping to carry the cavalier forward, bandaging arrow wounds, carrying water to a dying Indian. He remembered the same flash of pale gold on the head of a small boy climbing the rigging of a ship with a white cat at his belt. He had seen it again on the head of a taller boy tied to an Iroquois barricade. He felt the lashings come apart under the edge of his knife. He remembered a light-haired young man, dressed like an Indian, running to touch off a cannon at Quebec to salute his master's ship. He could see Tom standing open-mouthed because he—Champlain—had shot the great rapids that might lead them both some day to China.

It had never occurred to him that Tom would not be at his side when he needed him. He had been there, Champlain knew, when he had tried to persuade the chiefs not to retreat. Then the Indians had rushed past him yelling, chased by a small party of Iroquois who had sallied out of the fort. He had used his arquebus and rescued two Hurons who were in danger of being captured. Then all the Hurons had run off into the woods. He had shouted at them until his throat had almost burst. They had only yelled and whooped at each other. No one listened to his orders. His voice could not be heard.

He had no voice, he realized. That was why he could not make them hear. Tom was his voice and he was gone.

The Iroquois have him, he thought. My poor Thomas! And I can help him no more than a papoose. Perhaps when Etienne comes back...

But Etienne did not come back. Savignon became Champlain's interpreter. Through him Champlain tried to persuade the Hurons to return with him to the Iroquois country, to finish the battle so foolishly thrown away, to rescue or ransom Tom and Etienne.

It was no use.

"Captain Darontal says Tom and Etienne not prisoners now. Says Iroquois killed them long ago," Savignon reported.

It must be true, Champlain thought.

He had seen what had happened to the Iroquois prisoners they had brought with them from the battle. He knew all about fingernails torn out, burns made by heated hatchets, bleeding scalps. There were times when he despaired of ever making Christians of these savages. This was one of the times.

He had better return to Quebec. The river would soon be frozen. He asked Darontal to give him canoes and guides. The Captain said courteously that it would be sad for Champlain's friends if he left so soon. Would he not stay—now that his knee was so much better—and help them in the great deer hunt? The ice would not come yet, a little snow now and then, not cold enough to freeze the rivers yet.

It was a refusal, Champlain knew, though a polite one. He continued to ask for guides and canoes and Darontal continued to sidestep the subject. At last Champlain understood that he would have to winter with the Hurons.

"They need you and your thunder tubes if Iroquois come," Savignon told him. "Captain has cabin ready for you, parched corn, smoked fish, squashes. Not like Paris—France. No parsley, no lemons, no wine. I will bring you a kitten to catch mice."

Champlain had just moved into the cabin when the Hurons set out for the great deer hunt. He was still limping a little but he went with them.

"It is," he wrote, "esteemed the most noble hunt. We went first to a lake where I killed with my arquebus many ducks and geese, which we ate while we were waiting to find the deer. At last we reached the right place. Our captain had sent twenty-five men ahead. They had built three cabins out of wood and filled the chinks with moss. In a forest of firs, they fenced in a triangle, open on one side. The fenced sides were of stakes eight feet high, and close together. These fences were fifteen hundred feet long.

"At the point of the triangle they left an opening five feet across. It widened out into a small, fenced area. This they hid partly with boughs. In ten days the whole thing was ready.

"The next morning, half an hour before dawn, we set out more than a mile from the triangle. The Indians walked forward, some distance apart, at a slow pace, striking two sticks together. The deer went ahead. They could not leap the fences so they bounded along towards the small enclosure. Hidden near its opening sat men with bows, ready to let fly and roaring like wolves. Wolves eat deer. They are so frightened by the noise that they enter the little door and are easily captured.

"In the thirty-eight days we were there we killed a hundred and twenty deer in this way. The Indians also snared some. They save the fat for winter use. It is their butter. The skins are made into garments."

They waited for frost to make their journey home easy. On December 4th, lakes, ponds and marshes were frozen hard enough for the journey. The Indians carried loads of a hundred pounds each. Champlain was ashamed of carrying only twenty and finding it heavy. It did not occur to him that he was almost fifty years old and still recovering from a severe wound. Sometimes he pulled a toboggan on which some of the frozen deer meat was carried.

Toboggans, however, ceased to be of use when there was a four-day thaw. Suddenly they seemed to be walking on a road of splintered glass that broke under their feet at every step. Soon they were sinking in melted snow up to their knees, then to their waists. Snowshoes were so heavily loaded with snow that at every step it seemed as if their legs were being torn off. A man who tripped on a buried log or rock would lie in the snow and mud unable to move. Yet they struggled on through bogs, through pine forests full of blowdowns, across brooks, wet to the knees all the time.

About December 20th they reached Darontal's village. They found Captain Iroquet there. He had brought his son, who had been clawed by a bear. He had hoped to find Tom Lee to cure his son, Iroquet said. Missing Tom more than ever, Champlain did what he could for the young man. He was glad when he could turn the case over to the medicine man.

CHAPTER 13

DANCE ON SNOWSHOES

Among the Iroquois at the fort had been a small group of visiting warriors from the western shores of the Lake of the Iroquois. They stayed for some weeks after the battle was over, feasting, hunting, and dancing and telling each other stories about how many Hurons they had killed in the battle. They had been entertained by the torture of the Huron prisoners but they had not tortured their own prisoner much yet—a few handfuls of blond hair yanked out, a burn from a heated axe here and there, that was all. They were saving him until they got back to their own country where the whole tribe could enjoy the sport.

The young Indian who had taken him prisoner was wearing Tom's belt from which hung his case of surgical knives. While they sat around the fire at night, Onienta—that was his name—polished the knives, laughing as he did so. They would be just the thing for cutting chunks out of the prisoner's arms, he thought. He had once seen a very fine torture during which pieces of the prisoner were cooked on the fire beside him and he was made to eat them. He also had other plans he enjoyed thinking about.

It had taken the prisoner a long time to get over the blow on the head Onienta had given him with his stone axe. For a while he did not seem to know where he was. Now that they were traveling towards their own village he seemed to understand things better. Onienta was not even sure he knew whose prisoner he was. He decided to make it clear.

"You are my prisoner," he said. "I am called Onienta."

The prisoner said politely that it was a good name for the season. Onienta means snow and it was falling fast that day.

He smiled so cheerfully that Onienta, who had been thinking of yanking out some more of his hair, instead asked, "What is your name?"

"Thomas," the prisoner said.

"What were you doing in our country?" Onienta asked.

Tom Lee told him. Onienta found that the story made the journey go fast. He was a very young warrior and this was his first prisoner. He decided not to pull out any more of his hair at present. That would be fun, he thought generously, for the squaws and the children, especially his little brother. He wished to do the torture exactly right. There must be the correct songs and dances and the right jokes. Since the prisoner seemed brave and uncomplaining it would probably be proper to eat his heart. He must consult his uncle the medicine man about that. Perhaps a French heart ought not to be eaten.

Tom Lee understood a good many of these thoughts without their being spoken. He knew that when they reached Onienta's village, the torture would begin in earnest. There was little use in trying to escape. Onienta seemed to sleep with his black eyes open but even if he could avoid that rattlesnake gaze, he could not live long in the woods without food or weapons. He would only starve and freeze. He knew that Jean Nicolet, Champlain's best interpreter, had once lived on the bark of trees until at last he met some friendly Indians. If Tom met Indians, they would be Iroquois.

For the honor of France, Tom Lee decided, he would do what he could to hold out, he would use what courage he had as long as it lasted.

He wondered about Etienne. Had he too been captured? Was that why he had not brought the Carantouans in time for the battle? If he was a prisoner, Tom was sure his courage would see him through. Whatever you thought about Etienne—many people called him a rascal and hated his swaggering ways— there was no doubt about his courage. Tom wished he was as sure of his own.

Tom could not remember how many days they had been traveling; a week perhaps, he thought. Since the ground was hard and snow-covered and the rivers frozen, they were able to follow an almost straight course northeast. They had given him snowshoes. Onienta at times had let him help pull the toboggan with its load of French merchandise.

On their way to the fort, Onienta and his friends had held up a party of Hurons and taken their load. There were too many of them to take as prisoners so they had killed them. This was the best way to get red cloth coats and sharp axes, much easier than traveling five hundred miles with a bundle

of beaver skins, bargaining with stingy traders and then paddling five hundred miles back. Just wait at the portages. Let
someone else paddle his arms off. Onienta explained this view
of how to succeed in business to Tom as they pulled together
on the toboggan rope.

He had, he added, a fine present for his mother, three spoons,
not birch bark. Three spoons of a shining metal like dark ice.

Dark ice, pulling a toboggan... what was it that these words
made Tom think of? He didn't know—except that there was
ice in it.

Of course there is ice in it, he thought wearily. You don't
pull a toboggan over wild strawberries.

He wondered what those dark ice-colored spoons were
made of. Pewter probably.

Tom wished he were back at the habitation at Port Royal.
He made his first spoon there for the Good Time Order, he
remembered. You heated the pewter in a little iron ladle.
While it was heating you smoked the mold carefully. Then
you fastened it together and poured in the metal. In a few
minutes there was a spoon ready with the French shield at
the top of it. As soon as you filed off the rough edges, you
could eat with it. When spoons broke, you just melted them
up and cast them again.

He went on thinking about the pewter. It was a way to keep
from thinking about his master—much. He could keep his
courage up if he did not keep wondering about Champlain.
Was he alive? Had he been captured? Were they torturing him?
He could still hear him shouting in French to the Hurons as
they ran away from the fort. The last thing Tom remembered,

he was running towards Champlain to try to speak to the Hurons for him.

That must have been when Onienta hit him on the head with his stone axe. He had thrown it away, he told Tom, because now he had a French one. It was Tom's, his name was on the handle. Onienta had picked up a good bow and a quiver of arrows outside the fort after the battle. Those would be a present to his brother, he said.

"How old is your brother?" Tom asked.

Onienta thought a moment, then held up nine fingers.

"You have sisters? A mother and father?"

"No sisters. My father was killed by Hurons long ago. I have my mother. She is quite old. My uncle is the chief."

"You learned your skill in hunting from him?"

"Yes, and in war," Onienta said. "To make war on the tribes who killed my father and took my mother and brother prisoners. You chose the wrong friends, Man of Iron."

"How did you save your mother and brother?" Tom asked.

"You ask too many questions. Pull the toboggan," Onienta said scowling.

They went on in silence. They were near the end of the line of steadily moving figures. The snow was frozen to a thick crust here. Their snowshoes crackled on it and the toboggan moved with a scratching noise. The sun had gone down in a clear yellow sky. It would have been dark except for the sizzling green flash of the Northern Lights.

We must be near the village, Tom thought. We made camp before sunset the other nights.

He found that his teeth were chattering and knew it was

not because it was so cold but because the village was near. He scooped up some snow and ate it. The chattering stopped.

Now he must think of warm things so he could walk in like a Man of Iron, not like a shivering coward.

So he thought of ships' cabins with hot spiced wine on the tables, of stifling afternoons on the portages with clouds of black flies waiting like Iroquois to attack you, of fire blazing in the great hall at the habitation and his master reading beside it.

His teeth started clicking again. He had not meant to think of Champlain but his thoughts always led to him.

Onienta would hear the click. Tom began to whistle softly, trying to picture ladies in silks and satins dancing in a hot scented room with blazing candles shining on their curls.

"What is that music, Man of Iron?"

"An air of our King, Louis Thirteenth," Tom answered, changing to the minor and moving his feet to match it.

"Probably," he said half aloud, "no one has ever danced a gavotte on snowshoes in Canada before," and started whistling again.

An Indian in front grunted: "Too much noise."

Tom stopped the tune but there was still dance music coming across the snow, music of feet moving up and down in rhythm, rattling pebbles, shouts. He knew what those shouts meant. The first of the returning warriors had arrived.

The village was much like the Huron villages he had seen, more strongly fortified perhaps, but with the same palisades and gutters, the same long houses. It was breathing out its smoke through the roof openings. He knew well what it would be like inside—dogs putting their noses into cooking pots, women dancing with wailing papooses on their backs and stirring the *sagamité*, the medicine man rattling his tortoise shell, children yelling, kittens chasing their tails...

Only there won't be any cats. Poor Minette. He should never have taken her away from Quebec. Oh well—cats like places better than people. She was happy enough in Darontal's lodge. So many mice...

They were inside the third palisade now. The noise kept getting louder and louder as more people learned of the victory. Men were waving scalps they had taken. The chief was shouting that they had chased a thousand Hurons and a hundred Men of Iron into the woods. He imitated a Frenchman running in his heavy armor and everyone laughed.

Another voice yelled: "Onienta has a prisoner! Onienta has taken a Man of Iron with his axe of smooth stone!"

There was a great rush towards the place where Tom was standing. They crowded around him thumping his steel corselet, pulling at the crimson cloth of his sleeves and his doublet. He was almost stifled by the sweet, smoky, oily Indian smell.

"Do not touch my prisoner," Onienta said importantly. "He will make plenty of sport for us after we have eaten. This Man of Iron sings. He also dances. On snowshoes. Will you dance for us, Man of Iron?"

"With pleasure," Tom said.

He clicked his heels together, pretended he was sweeping off a beaver hat, putting his hand over his heart.

"Our uncle is kind," Onienta said.

Well, Tom thought, at least they call me uncle.

He knew it was a title of respect. They would not have used it for a coward.

Onienta went on courteously: "Our uncle must be tired after his long journey. He must rest his feet so he can dance well."

Two of Onienta's friends grasped Tom under the arms and held him up with his feet a foot from the ground while Onienta bound him to the palisade.

"Now our uncle can rest," Onienta said.

Strangely enough, Tom did rest. The noise from the feasting Iroquois came in dizzy waves to his ears, then faded out. His head fell forward. He slept.

When he woke, the victory banquet was still going on. A big fire had been kindled near him. A ring of Indian girls, loaded with *matachias*, danced around it. The firelight shone on their bracelets and necklaces. One had a square of deerskin on her back so thickly sewn and fringed with beads that it must have weighed more than a pound.

These girls were all handsome and graceful. Yet soon, Tom knew, they would be wrinkled toothless old hags. There seemed to be nothing in between. Except Moon Rises, he thought. She was the mother of two sons but she had not looked old. That was what pulling the toboggan and Onienta's saying "dark ice" had brought to his mind—the afternoon when he had pulled her and Small Arrow to the habitation on the toboggan. Now it all came back to him, the breaking ice, his snowshoes on the ice cake, his wet clothes freezing, Small Arrow's howling and his mother bearing her pain in silence. Etienne going off into the dark, singing, with the deer slung over his shoulder. How cold it was that night...

His teeth began to chatter again, not from cold. There was plenty of warmth from the fire where the girls were dancing. He saw the hatchets heating on it.

At another fire a man was scraping the last of the *sagamité* out of the kettle. The half-starved dogs at once began to fight over which should lick the kettle. Small boys were throwing snowballs and wrestling in the muddy snow. One of them had a bow and a quiver of arrows. He sent an arrow whistling past Tom's ear.

Tom saw Onienta take the bow away. This must be the small brother who was to have the Huron bow for a present. He was roaring like a panther and biting Onienta's arm. American children, as Tom's master and other visitors from overseas often noticed, were badly brought up. They had no respect for their elders. How restful it was in France, where children were taught to be seen and not heard—and how dull for the children!

Onienta had thrown his brother into a mud puddle. He still had the bow in his hand as he came up to Tom.

"Would my uncle like to dance a little now?" he asked.

Tom wondered who had taught him to bow almost like a Frenchman. His feathered head nearly touched his knee. He was dressed in his best bead-and-quill-trimmed deerskins with a cloak of beaver. His face was freshly painted and his hair shone with sunflower-seed oil. The two young men who had helped tie Tom up were with him. They were also handsomely dressed.

They cut the thongs with which they had bound him with one of his own knives. He tried to stand but his feet were so numb that he fell to the ground, sprawled in the mud and trampled snow. There was laughter all around him. The blood started to flow into his feet again. It prickled painfully but he managed to stand up.

"Fasten on my uncle's snowshoes," Onienta said to his friends. "He wishes to dance."

They bound the shoes on his feet. Then they tore off most of his clothes. One of them tried to put on his steel corselet but it was too small for him. He threw it to the ground. It struck a stone and clanged loudly.

"Dance for us, uncle. Sing us the music to which your King dances," Onienta said.

He picked up the corselet and beat on it with a stick.

So it has begun, Tom thought.

He started to sing the air of the gavotte and to walk through the steps, bowing to an imaginary partner. She was, he saw to his surprise, Hélène de Champlain, grown from a pink-faced, plump little girl to a pretty young woman, elegantly dressed. He turned her around under his arm, smiling down at her.

How lucky she is shorter than I am! he said to himself. He took his imaginary beaver off again and pressed the plumes against his heart, bowing. How clever she is not to step on my snowshoes!... Is this the way the gavotte goes?... I never danced except on Pontgravé's ship to Etienne's zither...

The Indians laughed till they cried but after a while they lost interest.

"My uncle has danced enough. He must not tire himself. My uncle's face looks hot. We must cool him." Onienta said.

They dragged him to the pond, where the water showed black through melting ice and threw him into it, snowshoes and all. The edge of the ice cut and bruised his shins. The pond was deep enough so he could have let himself drown.

That would be the easy way, he thought, but something would not let him follow it. The ice kept breaking as he grasped it but he reached the shore.

"Are you cold, uncle? Yes, our uncle is cold. See, he shivers. We must warm him a little. Let us come near the fire, uncle."

He walked towards it with his head up. They bound him again, this time to a birch sapling. They had a cord of hemp bound to the top of the tree. It was long enough to reach to the other side of the fire. When Onienta and his friends pulled hard on the cord, they could pull Tom almost into the fire. Then they would let go suddenly and the tree would snap back sharply. This sport went on for a long time. All the young braves had a turn at it. He had seen no older warriors yet.

They must be smoking in council, he thought. They'll come later.

He had become quite used to being pulled into the fire. It did not hurt him. His long hair fell forward and was singed at the ends. The smell choked him. His back ached from being snapped through the air. That was all.

"Our uncle is still cold," Onienta said. "We must warm him better."

Now! Tom thought.

He put his chin up, squared his shoulders.

The hatchets must be red-hot now.

They cut him first with his own knives. He felt the blood pumping and gushing down his arm.

"I'll bleed to death. Good. It won't be long now."

He felt something touch his leg, a feathery touch, so gentle, so soft that it seemed like the touch of Minette's tail. He looked down.

An enormous white cat with pink ears and green eyes that flashed gold in the firelight was walking around him, purring, brushing his legs with his fluffy tail. A smaller cat, also white, was stepping daintily towards him through the snow.

Out of the crowd of fighting children, Onienta's small brother came running. He snatched up both cats, one under each arm, and stood looking up at Tom.

Tom smiled down at him from his birch tree.

"Small Arrow!" he said gently.

Suddenly there was silence around him. Onienta came towards him, hatchet in hand. The crowd had stopped yelling. They made two lines between the birch tree and the door of one of the long houses. Three figures came out of the house into the blaze of the firelight—an old man in a beaver robe, a much younger man in deerskins with eagle feathers stuck in his oiled topknot of hair, and a woman, neither a pretty girl nor a wrinkled hag, but a tall, handsome woman who moved in a stately way in spite of a very slight limp.

She smiled up at Tom as if they had met only yesterday, then said quietly to Onienta, "Put down the hatchet, my son. This is your brother."

CHAPTER 14

BIRCH-BARK CANOE

IT WAS when he heard Moon Rises speak that Tom had fainted. When he became conscious, he was lying on a bed in the long house. It had been made soft and warm for him with skins and furs. Moon Rises had fastened a tourniquet around his arm. The bleeding had stopped.

"As you taught me to do, Tom Lee," she said, with the gentle smile that had not changed.

The two cats lay beside him, sleeping but twitching their tails in their sleep.

Dreaming of mice. He smiled but he did not speak. There was no need of talk between him and Moon Rises.

He lay on his bed in the long house for many days and nights. Often he did not know night from day. He burned with fever or shook with chills. He had a cough that seemed to tear him to pieces. Every breath he drew was a stab of pain under his ribs. They were broken, he supposed. There was not much to do about broken ribs except to wait until they mended. If only the cough would stop—but it grew worse.

The old chief and medicine man, Moon Rises' uncle, came and squatted beside his bed, talking to his stone. It was a flat oval gray-green stone.

Like those on the beach at Iron Bound, Tom thought, and felt himself tossed in a canoe by the gray-green water of Frenchman's Bay. He was often in a canoe, those smoky, feverish nights. He tried to paddle up waterfalls like hills of green ice and snow. He shot down rivers that were black snakes, twisting between black cliffs. He tried to drink the black water but it slipped away leaving his canoe in the mud.

His master was with him. "Speak to them, Tom," he said and Tom saw that what he had thought were white birches were Indians in white doeskins. They all had hatchets in their hands and the hatchets were all red-hot.

He heard his own voice say, "My master, Samuel Champlain of Brouage, gentleman, Governor of all Canada, says..."

He turned to Champlain but his master had vanished. He called and called to him, his cough choking him, his breath coming in great gasps, but his master never answered.

The old medicine man said to Moon Rises, "My stone says we must have dances and feast for him at once. The dance of the gifts. Next the fire dance. Then an eat-all feast."

So the long house was filled with dancers. They brought presents and piled them on his bed—furs, belts and collars of porcelain beads, hatchets. The women brought their precious French kettles. Small Arrow brought the cats. Onienta brought Tom's own knives, well polished, in their own case. The medicine man and the other chiefs of the tribe danced around the fire rattling their tortoise shells.

The young men rushed in for the fire dance. There were hideous masks on their faces and they rushed through the house snatching coals from the fires and throwing them everywhere. The old women, always terrified of fire, ran after them putting out the fires that started. Some of the young women joined the dance. One had a bearskin on, head and all. The bear's head was over hers and she growled like an angry bear. To the medicine man's disappointment, Tom still coughed and gasped for breath and called for his master.

"We must give the feast," the medicine man said to Moon Rises. "While you are preparing it, I will give him a steam bath."

They put him into a tent, set up over a pit with heated stones in it. Onienta was with him and kept dashing water on the stones. Clouds of steam rose, filling the tent. Suddenly Tom found he could breathe without coughing. They kept bringing more hot stones and Onienta kept the steam rising. When they told him the feast was ready, Onienta wrapped him in robes of beaver and carried him back to his bed.

There was venison grilling on the fires in the long house and *sagamité* was hot in the kettles. Moon Rises had brought out corn that had been buried in the mud for months, a great delicacy. There was fish caught through the ice, salt meat stolen from a Huron canoe and squashes baked in the embers. They had even killed a bear they had been fattening for some special occasion and they broiled bear steaks over the coals.

The tribe would be hungry for weeks after this feast but at present they must eat it all, every grain of corn, every fish scale. If they did, they told Tom, he would get well.

The medicine man set a splendid example by stuffing himself

with everything in sight. The guests all did the same, snatching food from the kettles, gobbling it down as fast as they could and going back for more. Only Moon Rises and her brother, who were the hosts, ate nothing but waited on their guests.

Soon there was nothing left. When the medicine man squatted by Tom's bed again and talked to his stone, he said his patient was better. Strangely enough Tom was better, though too weak to move. The next morning his cough was almost gone. He no longer felt as if his ribs were tearing his lungs to pieces.

He remembered only snatches of the night before—the steam from the hot stones, the terrible grinning masks, Small Arrow bringing in the cats. The cats were not the kind of presents that stayed where they were put—they had gone off on a mouse hunt—but the bed was still heaped with the other presents, furs, kettles, *matachias*.

He asked Moon Rises where the things came from. She told him that the medicine man had ordered the people to bring him their best things in case his illness was caused by longing for something.

On top of a heap of beaver skins was a small birch-bark canoe, a foot long perhaps. He picked it up. It was almost too heavy for his thin hand, a hand that looked as if it were made of wax. There were three figures in the canoe, two with paddles in their hands, one sitting in the middle. This figure had a white face and some of Tom's hair glued to its head. The canoe was as neatly and strongly made as a real canoe.

"I think you made this," Tom said to Moon Rises. "Does it mean what I think it does?"

"Yes," she said. "You shall go to your master. I heard you

calling for him. He is alive and in Darontal's village. He will go to the rapids in the spring. I knew what would make you well. Onienta has a Huron canoe. When the ice is gone, you shall go, in your own canoe, to take the place of the one we lost on our journey when you brought us home."

He tried to thank her but she had gone.

He grew strong quickly after that day. When the ice went out, he was able to paddle with the others. There were ten canoes in the party, all but Tom's the clumsy elm-bark kind. Tom traveled with the young chief, Moon Rises' brother, and with his nephew Onienta. To his surprise and relief they did not taunt him with the weakness he had shown by fainting and by his illness.

Onienta once remarked, when there was a dance one evening around the fire, "My uncle danced well on snowshoes," and that was all that was ever said on the subject.

Like almost all the Indians Tom had known, Onienta never complained of the hardships of the journey but was cheerful and gay whatever happened.

Once Tom said to him, "Tell me how it is that you and all your tribe can suffer so many hardships and never complain."

Onienta smiled and said, "Our chiefs teach us that if we complain about a misfortune, we suffer it twice—once when it happens, again when we complain about it. They tell us it is better to say nothing and be ready to meet what comes next."

As my master does, Tom thought. As Etienne does, or did, he added with a cold shiver running through him.

The Iroquois had told him that Etienne had been taken

prisoner on his way to the Carantouans. When they last heard news from the tribe that had captured him, they were having great sport burning him with hatchets.

"No doubt he is dead by now and his scalp is hanging at someone's belt," Onienta said, and then asked what color Etienne's hair was.

"Black, like yours," Tom said.

"A common scalp then, not the color of the sunflowers," Onienta said.

He seemed pleased at least that no one else had a blond scalp in his collection. Tom's scalp still prickled at such remarks, of which there were a good many, plenty in fact.

They had fine weather for their journey down the Lake of the Iroquois.

"I remember these mountains to the east," Tom said. "That one on our right is like a lion asleep with its head in its paws... What is a lion? Oh, a very large fierce cat, bigger than a catamount with a great mane of hair and a terrible roar. My master and I called the mountain *Le Lion Couchant,* which means a lion lying down. The one to the left we called the Sleeping Warrior. See, there is his forehead, then his nose, his long upper lip and his chin. Even in his sleep he thrusts his chin out to show his courage. Small Arrow and I called this side of Lake Champlain *Verts Monts.*"

"What does Champlain mean?" asked Onienta.

"Why—a level field, I suppose," Tom said.

"And you call our lake, with the mountains on both sides of it, after a level field!" the chief exclaimed.

"No," said Tom. "I called it for a man."

"Just a man?"

"Just a man—who has shown what a man can be," Tom said.

They found a party of Iroquois camped near the chestnut trees. They had a white cat and three white kittens with them.

"Minette's descendants!" Tom said to Onienta and added to himself, I must go back and see her next winter.

Most of the elm-bark canoes left them at the northern end of the lake but one went all the way with them to where the river of the Iroquois met the St. Lawrence. Onienta and his uncle would go back in this canoe to meet the rest of the party. They all risked their lives, Tom knew, to help him reach the St. Lawrence.

When he tried to thank them, they said cheerfully that it was nothing.

"You saved my mother and Small Arrow," Onienta said. "You are my brother."

In the elm-bark canoe were some of the presents Tom had been given when he was ill. He had managed to return the French kettles and the hatchets and the *matachias* but he had accepted the furs and his own surgical knives and the small canoe Moon Rises had made. He offered furs to his friends as a farewell present but they would not take them. At last he persuaded Onienta to accept one of the surgical knives. Perhaps it was the one with which Onienta had slashed his arm, Tom thought.

Onienta was probably thinking the same thing but they only smiled at each other without speaking. Tom got into his canoe. The Indians all raised their paddles in the air. The blades shone in the sun for a moment like slender fans of gold.

Then they dug deep into the green water. With the paddles

leaving deep whirlpools behind them, the heavy canoe moved upstream. Tom watched it disappear around a wooded point. As he turned the bow of his own canoe towards the sparkling blue St. Lawrence, he felt strangely lonely.

Near the island of Montreal there were several barques anchored. Farther up the river, near the foot of the rapids of La Chine, dozens of Indian canoes were pulled up on shore. Smoke rose from many fires and kettles were steaming. The French were giving a *tabagie* for their Algonquin and Montagnais customers. No Hurons had come yet.

Out in the stream, Indian guides were having a canoe tournament. One girl would sit in the stern and steer. Another would stand in the bow with her paddle pointed at another canoe. The game was to knock a bow paddler out of her canoe or—better still—to upset the whole canoe. When this happened there were squeals and shrieks of pleasure from the victors. Sometimes the girls, looking like seals in the water, swam the canoe to land. Sometimes they turned it right side up and, by tipping it back and forth, got most of the water out of it, climbed back in and went on with the game.

Tom landed and watched the dancing for a while. He saw no one he knew. At last he felt a blow between his shoulders that almost knocked him over. He turned around and found himself looking into Pontgravé's fat ruddy face. The old captain's hair and beard were white now but his voice was as loud as ever.

"Your master, Malouin! Where's your master?" he bellowed. "These Basque liars as usual are saying he's dead but I wouldn't believe them. Except Jean Nicolet heard it too."

Jean Nicolet, a tall thin grave-looking young man, came running forward eagerly. "Where is he?" he cried.

Tom was about to tell them that he did not know, and why, when he heard a great shout from the shore. All the Indians were running for their canoes. Whooping and screaming, they began to paddle upstream. With Nicolet's help, Tom launched his canoe and they paddled hard after the others.

Where the rapids boiled above the falls, they could see, spinning, whirling, darting, the Huron canoes. Heavy with their loads of furs, they rode low in the water. Figures looking as if they were carved out of dark copper stood in the bows. Flashing paddles guided them over hidden rocks and past foaming green whirlpools.

Tom and Nicolet were soon in the front ranks of the welcomers, clapping their hands against their mouths and yelling as loud as any Algonquin, striking their paddles against the sides of the canoe. Soon the leading Huron canoe was shooting the fall. It seemed to hang above them for a moment with Darontal's figure in the bow like a bronze tower. Then it flew down like a bird lighting, turning a little with the stream.

Behind Darontal, Tom saw a small man, a bearded man, sitting calmly in his wet shirt. He smiled and Tom knew the smile was for him, that both understood without more words what the other thought and had been thinking. He had, Tom saw, his notebook in his hand.

The Sieur de Champlain, gentleman, governor of Canada, had promised his Indian friends to meet them at the falls.

Here he was.

CHAPTER 15

TREACHERY

WHEN **C**HAMPLAIN returned to France in the late summer of 1616, he left Tom in charge of the Huron trade. People were beginning to call Tom and the other men who traveled through the wilderness, making friends with the Indians and bringing them to trade with the French, *coureurs de bois*. He and Jean Nicolet and the others were each paid a hundred pistoles a year to explore far places and to encourage the Indians to bring their furs to the trading place.

Champlain did not visit Canada again until 1618. With the Indians who came to the rapids that year was a familiar yet strange figure—Etienne Brulé, looking more like an Indian than ever with a badly scarred face and arms and body. Tom recognized his mocking smile and swaggering walk and brought him to his master.

"I asked him," Champlain wrote, "why he had not brought the five hundred Carantouans to help us in battle. He said in excuse that he and the twelve Hurons who went with him had reached the Carantouans after a hard journey. They had to avoid the Iroquois by taking a long route through bogs, forests and waste land. Crossing a meadow, they met some Iroquois, killed four and took two prisoners to the Carantouans. There were the usual delays, dances, *tabagies*, smoking together, speeches. Brulé tried to hurry them, saying that the battle would be over and the Men of Iron gone.

"In spite of all he could say, they were two days late reaching the Iroquois fort. The Hurons had gone. Brulé and the Carantouans went back to their village. They would not give him an escort to Darontal's village so he spent the winter exploring.

"He discovered a large river, which is called the Susquehanna. It leads towards Florida. He went all the way to the sea by it, finding there a mild climate where there was little snow. When he returned to the Carantouans, he was lost in the wilderness, wandering, starving for several days. He would rather face the Iroquois than starve.

"He met three Iroquois and made friends with them. They took him to their village. The people recognized him as a Man of Iron and rushed to see him. Soon they began to torture him, burning him severely with brands from their fires. A savage tried to snatch his holy medal, an Agnus Dei, from around his neck.

"Brulé said firmly: 'If you take it and kill me, all of your house will die suddenly.'

"The man still tried to snatch it and to continue his torture—they do not like to kill quickly—when the sky suddenly changed from clear calm to thick, black clouds, thunder and lightning so violent that all the savages were in terror and forgot their evil purpose. They did not unbind Brulé or even dare to approach him. This gave him a chance to speak to them. He told them God was angry with them for abusing him without cause. The chief then unbound him, took him into his house and treated his wounds."

The Iroquois let him go at last and he made his way to Darontal's village but Champlain had already left. Brulé became one of Champlain's *coureurs de bois* with a salary of one hundred pistoles a year. When the trading season of 1618 was over, he and Tom both went back to the Huron country, Tom to Darontal's village, Brulé to Toanche, the village of Captain Aenons.

Champlain did not come to Quebec again until 1620, yet Canada was never far out of his mind. Whether he was drawing a chart in a ship's cabin or waiting in the King's palace, trying to get some minister to understand the problems of the colony, the vast unexplored country was always in his thoughts. It breathed great winds and was scampered over by troops of animals. It could change as quickly from sunshine to storm as the Indians could veer from friendship and kindness to treachery and cruelty. This country did nothing by halves. The snows were the deepest, rains the wettest, thunder the loudest. It had the highest waterfalls, the fastest rapids, the hottest sun. Yet Champlain, whose virtues were patience and moderation, loved it.

At last in 1620 he persuaded his wife to make the voyage with him. Hélène de Champlain had three waiting women with her, as was proper to the Governor's lady. She had grown into a prim though pretty young woman. She had once been a Protestant but had been converted to the Catholic faith.

Religion was now her great interest. She would have entered a convent if Champlain had allowed her to do so.

Life in Quebec must have been hard for her. The habitation, as was usual when Champlain was away, had not been properly kept up. Gouty old Pontgravé, who had been left in charge, was more interested in eating, drinking, gambling and roaring out songs to the music of the zither than he was in seeing that the roof did not leak. You couldn't fix it in wet weather and in dry weather you didn't need to, he said.

One night—he told them, laughing till the tears filled his wrinkles—he had won an Indian's wife, his children, his canoe and all his clothes, in fact everything he had, at a game called Dish. In this game, he explained, you filled a dish with prune stones painted white on one side and black on the other. You jounced the dish and your opponent called out "black" or "white." If he called white and more stones were black side up, you won.

The Indian turned over his family and his *matachias*, his paddles and parched corn and beaver robe. When he staked his leggings and lost them, Pontgravé gave everything back to him and he was able to continue his journey.

There was great excitement among the Indians when they saw Champlain's wife. They had firmly believed that all Frenchwomen were hideously ugly and wore beards. The group that came to the habitation to meet Champlain fell into an awed hush when they first saw her and then burst into loud cheers.

There were even stranger passengers on the pinnace that had sailed up from Tadoussac—a pair of donkeys, the first ever seen in Quebec. When they set foot on shore, they brayed as loud as the Indians, who were terrified and ran for the wilds.

One asked Tom, who was on hand to meet his master, "Have the French brought these beasts to eat us or to rejoice us with these musical airs?"

Tom explained about donkeys but the Indians still jumped every time they brayed.

The habitation must have been a shock to Hélène. She had read her husband's book about his voyages. He had drawn a picture of the habitation and the engraver had made it look like a well-kept chateau. This shabby collection of buildings, huddled in the shadow of the great rock, with leaking roofs and a dirty courtyard, dead rosebushes and gardens full of weeds, looked, so Champlain wrote, like some poor abandoned place in the fields where soldiers had been camping.

The only neat-looking place was the farm of the Héberts, Canada's first real settlers. Champlain had asked the French minister to send him three hundred such families but the Héberts, who had come in 1611, were still the only ones.

Hélène liked the Indians. Tom used to help her talk with them when he visited Quebec. She never learned their language but she had her own way of making friends with them. She wore a small mirror around her neck on a chain, a fashion she had brought from France. She used to hold it out so that the Indians could look in it and see their faces in it.

They were delighted with this magic image and used to say to Tom, "See, she had our faces in her heart."

One face that she knew and was glad to see was Savignon's. She liked to talk about the wonders of Paris as well as he did.

She told him that he should be proud that the Indians still called him Paris-France. He could not have a finer name and only ignorant people would laugh at it. From that time on, Savignon cocked his beaver more rakishly than ever and added several new feathers to its plumage. He traded a beaver skin for red cloth and had the sleeves of his French coat lengthened so that he no longer showed five inches of bare wrist. It was still tight across the chest but as the buttons had long ago vanished into the place where buttons go, he no longer tried to fasten it anyway.

These visits to Quebec were almost as wonderful to Savignon as his trip to France. He talked about them for years afterwards. Champlain and his wife stayed in Quebec for four years. The habitation no longer looked like an abandoned camp. Gardens flourished again. Roofs let in no water. A new fort was built high on the rock above the habitation and a steeply twisting road led up to it. From it you could see far up and down the shining river. Any ship attacking Quebec would be within range of the fort's cannon, Champlain said.

Every spring the Indians of many tribes came to trade at Montreal. The *coureurs de bois* were earning their pay well, Champlain said. To Jean Nicolet, who had been to the western shore of the largest of the great lakes, he gave a Chinese robe of embroidered silk so that if Jean reached Cathay, he could be properly dressed as Champlain's ambassador to the Khan.

Champlain drew maps from the rough sketches his interpreters brought him. The original map might have been traced in mud or sand by an Indian on some distant lake shore, then transferred to birch bark and carried a thousand miles to Quebec in a bundle of furs.

Late spring and summer were the busiest times at Quebec. By the end of August summer visitors would all be gone, back to the wilderness or back to France. The habitation would settle down to the most beautiful time of the year, the brilliant golden days before snow and ice shut them in for another winter.

In the summer of 1623 Brulé guided a large party to the Hurons. There were eleven French laymen and three Recollet priests. One of them was Brother Gabriel Sagard, whose bright eyes looked eagerly at this country where everything was strange and new and who wrote about whatever he saw.

These were some of Champlain's happiest days. He was happy that the priests were carrying religion to the bronze-skinned subjects of his empire in the wilderness. At the moment it was a peaceful empire. Tom had been on a mission to the Iroquois to ask them to make peace with the French and with the Indian allies of the French. In the spring of 1624 there was a feast of peace and friendship between the Iroquois and the Hurons, Algonquins and Montagnais. The Iroquois came with thirty-five canoes full of furs. One of them was paddled by Onienta. Moon Rises and Small Arrow were among the party. Small Arrow was small no longer. He towered above Tom and was as fiercely painted as anyone.

With the Hurons came the Recollet priests. Brother Sagard sat in the great hall of the habitation and told all about their journey to the Huron country and back to Quebec. He had a pet muskrat with him. It lived in the sleeve of his gray robe, sometimes sleeping, sometimes looking out with bright eyes.

He told how Brulé had found some long tumbling rapids that led to a vast inland ocean. He was a fine explorer, Sagard said, but he had not helped the priests. He did not wish the Indians to settle down and learn to be Christians. He thought it was better for the fur trade if they went on running through the wilderness. He had not—Sagard said—helped the priests to learn Huron, in fact he purposely told them the wrong names for things so that the Indians would laugh at them. Sagard, however, was learning without Brulé's help and writing down the meanings of words with the idea of making a dictionary.

The Hurons evidently liked him. They all flocked to see him. He gave a feast for them at the house Champlain had built for the Recollets, with presents for everyone. The Huron Captain who had been Sagard's guide admired especially a large striped tomcat. Brother Gabriel said he might have him for his own.

The Captain was delighted. He thought that because the cat came when Sagard called, it understood French perfectly.

"Tell the cat," he said to Sagard, "that if he will let himself be carried back to my country, I will love him like my own son. Oh, Gabriel, tell him that he will have plenty to eat! You say he is fond of mice. We have any number, as you know."

So saying, he tried to grasp the cat, which spat, thrust out all its claws and scratched so fiercely that the Huron quickly let him go.

"Ho! Ho! Ho! So that's the way he treats me. Ongaron! Ortischat! He's ugly! He's bad! Speak to him, Gabriel! Tell him to be good!"

Brother Gabriel suggested that the cat would have to be carried in a bag or a box. The Captain went away and after a time came back with a cage neatly made of birch bark. After a struggle in which there were more scratches and spitting, the cat was shut in the box. The Captain had left a little window in the box for light and air. Through this he offered the cat some French bread left over from the feast. The cat ate it. He even purred a little and settled down in the box as the Captain went off with it in his arms.

All went well until they got back to the place upstream where the Indians' camp was. There was *sagamité* cooking in a kettle on the fire. The Captain offered the cat some as a treat.

It was too much.

The cat burst through the box as if it were paper and, yowling loudly, ran up a fifty-foot pine. No one could get him down. They tried calling him but—the Captain told Brother Gabriel— "There was nobody home. He does not know Huron and I do not speak French. We are sad to lose him and I think he is sad in that tree because he does not know who will feed him next."

"At least he knows he won't get *sagamité*," Tom said when Brother Gabriel told him about the cat.

After the Indians had left the camping place, Tom climbed the tree, being careful to talk French all the way up. He took an old deerskin shirt with him, put it over the cat's head and got him safely down. The cat seemed to be happy to get back to the habitation and French cooking but he went peaceably to Darontal's village with Tom.

Two years before, Minette had died at a great age, lying down to sleep on Tom's bed and not waking. No one would ever take Minette's place with Tom—she was his oldest friend—but the striped cat proved to be a good catcher of mice and moles. He held his own with the Huron dogs. He learned to sit quietly, looking wise, with his paws turned in when it was going to rain. He even learned to eat *sagamité.*

Brother Gabriel Sagard did not go back to the Huron country. The Recollets had decided they were too few and too poor to do the great work of bringing Christianity to the Indians. They decided to ask the Jesuits to help them in the work. When Champlain and his wife returned to France in 1624, Father Joseph Le Caron and Brother Gabriel went with them.

Six Jesuit fathers came out to Canada in 1625. Tom saw the first one arrive in the country of the Hurons. This was Jean de Brébeuf, a tall man of enormous strength, a strange figure to the Indians with his bushy black beard, his long black robe, his wide-brimmed black hat. He had already, with Brother Gabriel's help, learned some Huron words. On the long journey he had shown the patience and cheerfulness needed to make the Indians accept him as their friend.

Champlain did not come back to Quebec until 1626. As usual he found the habitation uncared for. Piles of boards meant for repairs lay just where they had been for two years, rotting from rain and snow. The gates of the fort were open. It was guarded only by hens. The hens squawked when Champlain appeared. They at least ran about busily. Soon others were doing the same.

He dreamed again one night, a dream he had had many years before, of a great city built at Quebec with shining church towers and handsome stone houses. He even wrote to King Louis about it and said he would call the city after him. To make the name sound properly majestic it would be in Latin—Ludovica. In the meantime he had the fort and the habitation repaired.

The Jesuits with twenty workmen were building a mission center, which they called Our Lady of the Angels. Already they were starting to teach the Indian children. Father Brébeuf himself had written hymns for them to sing. Champlain was happy about the work of the Jesuits but there were other things that troubled him greatly. Peace between the Iroquois and the other tribes had been broken, not through the fault of the French. Rivers and portages were no longer safe from the Iroquois. Hurons and Algonquins were captured, tortured and scalped. Their furs and their French merchandise were again being carried off to the Iroquois country.

Across the Atlantic, England and France were at war, seizing each other's cargoes, sinking each other's ships.

"They are no better than Iroquois and Hurons," Tom said to his master.

This was when he made his spring visit of 1628 to Quebec. The winter had been a bad one with starving Montagnais crossing on heaving ice cakes to beg for food. Champlain gave them what he could spare though his own provisions were running short. There was always a time in the spring when food was scarce. As soon as the ice went out, French ships with cargoes of food were always watched for eagerly. This year none came.

By the time Tom arrived, there were only four barrels of biscuit left with peas and beans. Nothing would ripen in the gardens for many weeks. The colony was living on fish.

"The English may have seized our ships," Champlain said to Tom and to another of his interpreters. This other man was, strangely enough, a Greek and was spoken of only as the Greek. "Dress yourselves as Indians—cover that hair of yours, Thomas—get down to Tadoussac. Bring me what news you can."

The trouble was already nearer than Tadoussac. At Cape Tourmente, only thirty miles down the river, the French had a settlement where they were beginning to keep cattle. There were good pastures there. Champlain had had barns built for winter shelter. It was already dark when Tom's canoe arrived at Cape Tourmente. They went ashore and asked Foucher, who was in command of the settlement, if they could sleep there that night. He gave them milk to drink, the first milk Tom had ever drunk in Canada, and showed them where they could sleep in the hay.

They were awakened by the sound of voices, English voices, coming from Foucher's house nearby.

"We must see what this means," Tom said to the Greek.

They slipped cautiously out of the barn. It was close to the river. There were six ships anchored off shore. English was almost a foreign language to Tom now but he understood when he heard the master of one ship call across to another, "They are taking enough time in there, to be sure. We ought to be getting up the river with the tide."

English ships! How could they get up the river in the dark? Who were the pilots?

These questions were soon answered. They had only to look in the window of Foucher's house.

Foucher and his men were backed up against the wall. The English soldiers had their muskets pointed at them. The pilots were standing beside the English commander.

They were Etienne Brulé and Nicholas Marsolet.

Tom had long known that Nicholas Marsolet would do anything for money, but Etienne! Etienne who was supposed to be finding the western road to China. Why was he lounging against a table laughing while Foucher stammered out, "Surrender? Of course we surrender! What can we do against you? Only I pray you, do not hurt any of my beautiful cows."

"We must go and warn my master," whispered Tom to the Greek.

In the darkness they found their canoe.

"We can't launch it here," Tom said softly. "We must get upstream."

They carried the canoe first through the woods then across meadows, then through woods again to the Quebec side of the cape. They were ready to launch it when they heard, from the barns, a great outburst of sound, shouts in both English and French, bellowing of cattle, then feet hurrying to the shore. Behind them there was smoke, a red glow and the terrible crackling noise of burning hay.

"Wait," Tom said to the Greek. "I am going back to see if I can find Foucher."

"You'll be captured," the Greek said.

"Oh, they won't bother about one Indian more or less just now," Tom said.

The English had killed all the cattle. They were loading the carcasses into their boats. In the firelight Tom saw Etienne, a dead calf slung over his shoulder, just as he might have carried a deer, stride down to the shore and get into a boat.

Etienne! He could still not believe it.

He could not see Foucher. They had probably taken him on board the ship. He circled the burning buildings and went back to the canoe. They had gone only a little way when they heard someone crashing through the bushes along the shore.

"Who's there?" called Tom.

"It's Foucher—take me, take me to Quebec. We must warn them."

They traveled the rest of the night. The tide helped them and there was no wind but when they reached Quebec, they could hardly have driven the canoe another mile.

Champlain's face was grim as he listened to Foucher's story of the arrival of the ships.

"I thought they were French," Foucher said. "Those who came ashore first spoke French, but they were traitors. The ships were English. Your interpreter Brulé, the one with the scars on his face, was one of the first ashore. Nicholas Marsolet from Tadoussac was with him. They told me they were going to Quebec with dispatches. While I was talking to them the English landed. They surrounded me and my men. We could only surrender."

Champlain said, "Etienne and Nicholas! I cannot believe it."

"They were there," Foucher said. "They helped the English burn our houses. They helped kill the cattle. The English took the meat to the ships. My beautiful cows! They even snatched the cap from the head of a little girl, the child of one of my men. They took the men on board the ships but in the hurly-burly I managed to slip away."

Champlain did not wait to hear more. He sounded the alarm, sent men to their posts, gave out arquebuses, powder and shot.

With his own hands he worked on trenches and barricades. He helped pile balls for the cannon. They had fifty barrels of powder, not enough for a long siege.

"But we can do something," he said to Tom.

On July 10th the English ships, all six of them, were seen from the fort, their white sails bright in the hot sun, coming up the river. They were larger than the barques and pinnaces the French used.

"It took clever pilots to show them the channels," Champlain said.

"Yes," said Tom.

They both knew who the pilots were.

"No doubt the English paid them well," Champlain said.

They saw a small boat leave the side of one of the ships. Tom went down to the landing place to meet it. Basque oarsmen were rowing it. Nicholas Pivert, one of Foucher's cattlemen who had been taken prisoner, was the messenger. He brought a letter from the commander of the fleet, David Kirke of Dieppe and England. Or was it Scotland? Tom was not sure but he remembered the five tall young Kirkes at Dieppe when he was a small boy. Like him they had an English father and a French mother. Only they had chosen to be English, as he had chosen to be French. Their choice was one they had a right to make.

But Etienne and Nicholas—traitors to Champlain as well as to their country—he could not bear to think of them.

David Kirke's letter was a courteous one. Tom managed to translate it to his master, though English had almost ceased to be one of his languages. Kirke said that since he was blockading the river, starvation would be the fate of Quebec. Champlain could, he said, surrender without loss of honor.

"I desire to avoid bloodshed," he wrote. "If you surrender this place with courtesy, you shall receive good treatment both as to your persons and your goods, which latter, on my hope of Paradise, I shall preserve as carefully as if they were my own. Awaiting your reply, I shall remain, sir, Your affectionate servant, David Kirke.

Champlain listened quietly to David Kirke's letter. He made no comment on it. He cut himself a new pen from a wild-goose quill. He tried it on a leaf from his notebook. When it suited his hand, he took a large sheet of his best paper and wrote quickly and firmly without blotting or scratching out a word. The sound of his pen was the only noise Tom heard in the great hall for a long time. At last he laid down his pen and gave the letter to Tom to read.

"Sir," his master had written. "We entertain no doubt as to the commissions you hold from the King of Great Britain. Great Princes always choose men of brave and generous disposition, amongst whom he has chosen you to fulfill the duty he has assigned you.

"It is true that the better a fortified place is provisioned, the better it holds out against the storms of time, nevertheless, a place can make good its defense when order is maintained. Since we have grain, Indian corn, peas and beans, not to mention what this country produces, and knowing well that if we were to surrender a fort and settlement conditioned as we now are, we should not be worthy of the name of men in the presence of our King, honor demands that we fight to the death. For these reasons I know that you will think more highly of our courage if we firmly await the arrival of yourself and your forces than if, in a cowardly fashion, we should abandon something so dear to us without first making proof of your cannon against a place, which I am confident you will judge, when you reconnoiter it, not to be so easy of access as perhaps you have been led to suppose; nor its defenders destitute of courage, seeing they are men who have tried their courage in many different places. Then, if the issue is favorable to you, you will have more cause, having vanquished us, to bestow your offers of kind treatment, than if without a struggle we should put you in possession of a place the preservation of which is our duty.

"We are now waiting from hour to hour to receive you and resist, if we can, the claims you are making to these places and I shall remain, Sir,

Your affectionate servant
Champlain"

Tom carried the letter down the cliff and gave it to Pivert. Then he went back to the fort and waited with his master for the English to fire or to try to land. There was no attack. When the tide turned, the English ships sailed off downstream.

Champlain watched the last of the sails disappear behind the big island where the wild grapes grew—Ile d'Orléans, he had named it.

He said with a twinkle in his brown eyes, "I think they wanted beaver skins, not honor and glory. It seems we are to have neither today."

They saw nothing more of the English ships but no French ships came either.

"We must feed ourselves without help from France," Champlain said.

Tom did not go back to Darontal's village that year. He stayed with his master and did what he could to help feed the garrison by working in the gardens, hunting and fishing. Champlain had seventy-five men to feed. He bought smoked eels from the Indians. There were beets, carrots, cabbages, about half a pound a week for each man. They dug Solomon-seal roots. They made *sagamité* with fish and boiled acorns in it. There were enough dried peas and beans so that each man had seven ounces a day. Champlain weighed and measured their rations with his own hands. They could not use much powder and shot. It had to be saved in case the English came back. Tom taught some of the soldiers to track the moose as the Indians did until it floundered in deep snow and they could kill it with arrows and spears. Sometimes when they caught no fish, they bought it from the Indians, even giving their coats in exchange.

On their scanty diet they were often so exhausted that cutting wood for the fires seemed an impossible task. Yet no one died of scurvy that winter and Pontgravé's gout was better. When spring came, they were still watching the river for sails.

On June 17th Father Brébeuf arrived from the Huron country. He brought some corn but not enough for the starving garrison. He reported that the Indians who had found the trading post at Montreal deserted were angry and had carried their furs back to their villages.

Champlain knew now that if the English returned he must surrender. They could not even live until the harvest, not to speak of another winter.

"Two days after Father Brébeuf appeared," Champlain wrote, "an Indian came running to tell me that there were three great English ships in the river. I was alone in the fort, some of my company having gone to fish, some to dig roots. At about ten in the morning my servant Thomas, arriving with four small bags of roots, told me he had seen the ships behind Point Levis. I put in order what little we had for defense. After conferring with the Jesuits, the Recollets and others of our company, we decided to ask for terms, if they were not satisfactory, to do what we could to show them they would lose men in a landing."

The sails of the three ships now showed in the river near the Ile d'Orléans. They stayed beyond cannon range. A boat carrying a white flag crossed the river. Champlain had a white flag run up above the fort. An English officer was soon briskly climbing the steep path up the rock. Champlain and his starving hollow-cheeked companions, bronze-skinned and white, received the messenger courteously. The letter, signed by Louis and Thomas Kirke, again offered honorable terms of surrender.

The Kirkes offered to transport Champlain, the garrison and the Recollets and Jesuits safely to France. Champlain and Pontgravé might carry their clothes, books, arms and their own furs. The soldiers might take one beaver skin apiece.

Champlain could only agree to these terms.

On July 20th, 1629, the Kirkes took possession of Quebec. English drums sounded. English soldiers marched into the fort. Louis Kirke tore down the shield with the French lilies

and nailed up the British lion and unicorn in its place. They hauled down the blue and white flag of France and ran up the British flag. When the red flag showed against the sky, the cannon on the rock were fired and the ships fired all their guns in answer to the salute.

Tom Lee was not in the fort. Champlain told him he could help most by going back to the Hurons.

"Keep them friendly to France," Champlain said, "for this will not be the end. The lilies will fly over the rock again. We have a good friend in France, Cardinal Richelieu. He will not see this empire lost to France. To you, Jean Nicolet, I say the same thing. Explore all you can to the west, both of you. When I come back, perhaps you can show me the road to China."

So it was from a canoe, on the river, that Tom and Jean Nicolet heard the guns of Quebec sound for a French defeat. Smoke puffed out from the English ships before the sound of their guns began to echo from the rock. For a moment the ships were lost in smoke. Then it thinned and was blown between them and the habitation.

Without speaking, Tom and Jean Nicolet--with his Chinese robe in his pack—dug their paddles into the water and started up the river.

CHAPTER 16

COUREUR DE BOIS

ON JULY 24th, 1629, Champlain was on an English ship sailing down the St. Lawrence. They met a French ship coming to the aid of Quebec but it was not strong enough to face the English guns. Her captain surrendered. He told the English captain that peace had been signed between England and France months before. The Englishman only stared coldly and refused to believe him.

At Tadoussac they found David Kirke, Admiral of a fleet of five large ships. His rear admiral was a French traitor, Jacques Michel. With him were Etienne Brulé and Nicholas Marsolet.

"When I saw them," Champlain wrote, "I said to them, 'God will punish you. To think of you, brought up from boyhood here, turning around and selling those who put bread into your mouths! You should have a horror of yourselves. Do you think you will be esteemed by the English? Surely not! They only make use of you. They know well that if some one offers you more money, you will sell them too. When they know the country, they will drive you away. People make use of traitors only for a time. You will be pointed at with scorn. People will say: "These are the men who betrayed their king and sold their country!" Better to die than to live so. You will always have a worm gnawing at your conscience."'

Both the traitors scowled sullenly and defiantly at Champlain. Then Brulé said with something of his old reckless gaiety, "Well we know that if they had us in France we would hang but we have made up our minds never to return. We'll manage to live just the same."

Marsolet added: "Don't forget we saved you from starvation by bringing the English up the river."

"What poor excuses!" Champlain said, turning away in contempt.

As he had said, the traitors were scorned by their new masters as well as by the French. They both soon disappeared. For a long time there was no news of Marsolet but Tom saw Brulé the next winter at Toanche. The Hurons there had called Brulé their brother but since he had betrayed Champlain, the looks they turned on him were no longer entirely friendly, Tom thought.

Perhaps they knew that a man who has once been a traitor finds treachery easier the second time. Perhaps they remembered that Etienne had lived with the Iroquois as their friend after he had been saved from torture by that convenient thunderstorm. Certainly, though they said nothing about him in Tom's hearing, they no longer thought of him as their brother.

Tom continued to go to the trading post at Montreal every spring to learn news of Champlain. He heard that the war was over and that Champlain would return but the years went by and the ships at the foot of the rapids were always English, never French. Darontal's village did not bring their furs to trade with the English but there were some Indians who did. Through them he heard that Quebec would be given back to the French soon but the day was long in coming.

It came at last, on April 18th, 1632, when Thomas Kirke yielded up the fort to a French commander. Tom visited Quebec soon afterwards. It was the first time he had seen the rock since he left it, veiled in cannon smoke, in 1629. The habitation had burned. Weeds and vines covered the spot where it had once stood. The great sundial must be somewhere in the ashes. Tom hunted for it but did not find it. The Recollets' chapel had disappeared. The Jesuits' house was standing but rotting away, its windows broken, its roof sagging.

When my master comes, it will be different, Tom thought.

In Paris, Champlain was busy. He published a book giving the whole history of his explorations up to 1632. He included in it a piece on the art of navigation called "The Good Navigator" and a list of Indian words given to him by Father Brébeuf. He made his will.

The King and Cardinal Richelieu had put him in absolute command of all trade with the Indians as well as making him again governor of all Canada. His faith in Richelieu was well placed. From now on the colony had plenty of men, arms and provisions. The Jesuits, including valiant Father Brébeuf, came to take up their mission again.

Champlain arrived at Quebec on May 22nd, 1633. He was not discouraged by what he found there. When was he ever discouraged? So, the habitation is in ashes? Well, a new warehouse will be built. When will it be begun? Why, now—before dinner.

When Champlain left Quebec he had vowed that when he returned—he said *when* always, not *if*—he would build a chapel in honor of Our Lady of Recovery. This soon began to rise on high ground near the fort.

Even before the warehouse was built, a hundred and forty Huron canoes, loaded with furs, arrived at the rapids of La Chine.

Tom Lee was there to welcome his master and to act as his interpreter. His master had changed hardly at all. Perhaps his hair and beard were a little more silvery than Tom remembered but he moved with energy and his brown eyes were as bright as ever.

He had never listened with such interest to the Indian speeches.

"Tell me every word," he would say to Tom and Tom would translate carefully, saying, "The chief speaks as follows, 'I am only a poor animal crawling on the ground. You Men of Iron are the great ones of earth. You make us tremble. I do not know how to talk before such great Captains. I am bewildered. I have no one to give me good counsel. My father died when I was very young. What shall I say?'"

"Tell him he speaks well," Champlain would answer. "I listen to his words with great pleasure."

Tom had to translate to his master a piece of news that troubled and frightened the Indians. They did not know what Champlain would do when he heard it. Champlain had heard it already but he listened with his usual attentive courtesy, watching the speaker's face.

Etienne Brulé had been killed in a quarrel with the men of

Toanche, his own village. His body had been eaten with the ceremonies appropriate to the occasion.

"Will the Men of Iron be angry with us because of what the men of Toanche have done?" the speaker, a Huron chief, asked. "We are ready to give many beaver to keep friendship between us."

"Tell him," Champlain said gravely, "that we ask nothing from them. When by treachery he helped the English take Quebec, Etienne Brulé ceased to be French. His death shall not hurt the friendship between us. We will trade our goods for your beaver. We will not accept them for the life of any man, friend or foe."

The Indians were pleased with this speech yet, as Tom told his master, they could not understand why he would not take the beaver.

"They cannot understand our ideas of punishment," he said. He told Champlain something that had happened with some Nipissing traders the day before.

"A little French boy who was beating a drum," Tom said, "accidentally struck one of the Nipissings, who was squatting close to the drum. His head began to bleed. He was angry. He and his friends came to me asking for presents, kettles and knives in return for the injury."

"What did you do?" Champlain asked.

"First I bound up his head. They always like bandages, as you remember. Then I said to him: 'Thou knowest our custom. We do not buy or sell justice. The child has done wrong. When one of our people does wrong we punish him. The child shall be beaten in your presence.' I had the little boy brought in.

When they saw we were in earnest, that our men had switches in their hands and were stripping this little pounder of drums and Indians, they began to pray for his pardon, saying: 'He is only a child. He has no sense. He did not know what he was doing!' As our men kept on taking off his clothes—the boy did not cry a tear or make a sound—the Indian stripped his own robe off his back and threw it over the child, then knelt down saying: 'Strike me if thou must, but thou shalt not strike him.' So the little one escaped without a blow, the switches were thrown in the fire and we ate our *sagamité* happily together."

Champlain had been chuckling and smiling over the story. He saw it all—the pink-cheeked, sturdy little drummer, the tall, bronze-skinned men with their painted faces—angry one minute, pleading for mercy for the boy the next.

"They are children," he said, "I love them in spite of their faults, as if they were my own children. I felt the same towards Etienne until he betrayed us. Whatever faults he had, I overlooked because I thought he was loyal and because of his great fortitude. No one, not even you, Thomas, not even Jean Nicolet, brought me better information. You know how good the maps he made for me have proved to be. But without loyalty what is a man? An Indian dog is better."

He was silent for a moment, then added: "I am sorry he is dead but a man should live so that when he is old he can sleep peacefully at night. For Etienne there could be no peace. He lived as a traitor to his King. He died as a traitor to his village. They condemned him, Nicolet says. Yet they loved him. Tell me again what Captain Aenons said when he asked for his bones, to bury them with those of his people."

Tom repeated what Darontal had heard Aenons say: "I took him into my canoe at Quebec, in the shadow of the rock. His stroke kept time with mine as we paddled up great rivers and through white water. He helped carry my canoe over long and rough portages. I brought him here. His bones are mine."

The trading, the speeches, the songs and the dances went on for days. There were more pipes smoked, more *sagamité* eaten, more Indian girls upsetting each other's canoes than ever before. Champlain was back in Canada and his children rejoiced.

Then one night, according to their custom, they disappeared as suddenly as a flock of Canada geese. Tom stayed long enough at the fort to see how life went on there. It was rather like being in a well-run school, he thought. At meals Champlain had someone read aloud, history at the noon dinner, stories from the *Lives of the Saints* at supper. The meals were good now. Each man was allowed two big loaves of bread a week, two pounds of bacon, one of salt codfish, two ounces of butter, oil and vinegar. The rest of the food came from vegetable gardens, from hunting and fishing.

The Angelus was sounded morning, noon and night for prayers and there was music—hymns sung by the Indian children from the Jesuit school, French songs sung by the soldiers. There were always Indians listening with delight to the music and the sound of bells.

Champlain's manner with them was playful and cheerful. "You always say jolly things to bring us cheer," they told him.

"One day," Champlain wrote, "I was in the chapel with

the Jesuit fathers when some Indians looked in the window. Enjoying their wonder at the place, I gave one of them a piece of candied citron. He, tasting it, cried out: 'Oh, how good it is!' and divided it with his friends."

When they asked what it was, he told Tom to tell them it was a French pumpkin.

"They were much astonished," Champlain wrote, "and told us that our pumpkins were wonderful. More and more came asking for some, saying they would like to taste it, so as to tell in their country about it. You can judge how all in the room began to laugh."

It was kindly laughter and the Indians joined in it. They kept asking Tom to give them seeds of French pumpkins to plant.

He and Jean Nicolet went far into the great lakes in the summer and late autumn of 1633. Nicolet was a good traveling companion of great endurance.

Tom said to him once, "Is it true that you once lived in the wilderness on the bark of trees for seven days?"

"No," said Nicolet. After a slight pause he added: "Seven weeks."

He had lived mostly with the Algonquins exploring their country. Now Champlain wanted him and Tom to go together and try to find that great river that Brulé had tried so long to find, the Mississippi.

The Indians told stories about it but it was always a little farther on, sometimes west, sometimes south. Tom began to believe it was only a dream. When the lakes and rivers began to skim over with ice, they had to turn back without finding it.

Nicolet still carried his Chinese robe in his pack in case they reached the land of the great Khan. He wore it several times when he sat and smoked with the chiefs of tribes along the lakes. He and Tom were both given the task by Champlain of keeping peace between these distant tribes and the Hurons. Perhaps the Chinese robe with its embroidery of flowers and birds helped their mission to succeed. When they visited Quebec in 1634 they were able to report peace along the lakes.

This year the Huron traders came all the way to Quebec. Tom counted more than six hundred of them. Some came to trade, bringing furs and tobacco. Some came to steal, more from the Montagnais and the Algonquins than from their fellow Hurons. It was considered proper to steal if you did not get caught. Some used their feet when their hands were being watched. Quarrels of course resulted and the interpreters had to straighten them out.

Some of the Indian visitors were simply sightseers. They came to enjoy the banquets and dances, to see Quebec, to gamble and win French goods from the traders. This meant more quarrels. The interpreters were usually glad when the trading fair was over.

Luckily it did not last long. The first day the Indians built their cabins. On the second day they sat in council with Champlain and the French officers at the fort. The third and fourth days they bartered their furs and tobacco for French goods—the cherished knives and kettles and hatchets, French coats, red cloth to make cloaks, beads to trim moccasins, arrowheads of iron.

On the fifth day they danced and feasted on a favorite dish—peas and prunes and French biscuit all boiled together in a kind of pudding. By the next day the river was as empty as if no paddle had ever made a whirlpool in it.

On the day of council that year Tom saw sixty tall chiefs climb the rock. They were splendid in their beaver robes. Their faces shone with red and yellow and white paint. No black—black was for mourning and war. Their hair shone with sunflower-seed oil. Some wore it hanging loose on their shoulders. Some in bristling ridges from their foreheads to their necks or in whatever was the latest style among the young men of the tribe.

Tom knew many of them and told his master from which villages they had come. Champlain himself recognized among the other chiefs men who had been with him in the attack on the Iroquois fort.

This year, after the exchange of presents and speeches, Champlain asked the Hurons to take Father Jean Brébeuf and two other Jesuit missionaries back to their country with them. The Hurons, after some discussion and some extra presents, agreed to do so.

Tom saw the fathers embark for their nine-hundred-mile journey. Father Brébeuf had taken it before but he faced it cheerfully—the thirty-five portages, the fifty or more times of wading barefoot over stones in rushing streams, dragging their empty canoes, the trips back to get their baggage and carry it overland. Often this meant several miles of pushing through underbrush, climbing over logs and rocks, being bitten by black flies and mosquitoes.

Brébeuf had written down a set of rules for his brother priests who had never made the trip: "Love the Indians like brothers with whom you will spend the rest of your life. Never make them wait for you in embarking. Take flint and steel to light their pipes and kindle their fires at night. These little services win their hearts. Eat their *sagamité* as they cook it, bad and dirty as it is. Fasten up the skirts of your cassock that you may not carry sand and water into the canoe. Wear no shoes or stockings in the canoe, only on the portages. Ask few questions. Bear their faults in silence. Be cheerful, always. Buy fish for them from tribes you pass. For this purpose carry beads, knives and fish hooks. In the canoe be careful that the brim of your hat does not annoy them. It is better to wear your nightcap. Remember it is Christ and His cross you are seeking. If you aim at anything else, you will find only affliction of mind and body."

Tom was at Ihonatiria when Father Brébeuf arrived. This was a new village. The inhabitants of Toanche had moved there after their village burned. At Toanche Father Brébeuf had found only the charred poles where the chapel had stood where he had taught for three years.

A crowd ran out from Ihonatiria to meet him yelling "Echon!"—their way of saying Jean. "Echon has come again!" they shouted as they saw the tall, blackbearded figure in the black cassock and the wide-brimmed black hat.

The whole village turned out to build him a house. It was thirty-six feet long and about twenty wide. Like any Huron house, it was built of saplings bent over and lashed together and covered with bark. The priests did things inside with tools they had brought that astonished the Indians. They divided it into three compartments, one for a storeroom, one for a living room and bedroom, one for a chapel. Each room had a wooden door, a great wonder. The chapel was more wonderful still with its sacred images and pictures, the altar and the chalice.

The greatest marvel of all was a clock that stood in the living room. Indian visitors would sit for hours waiting for it to strike. They thought it was alive and they asked what it ate. One of the Frenchmen for a joke would cry out "Stop!" just before the last stroke sounded. The Indians were sure it understood him.

"What does the Captain say?" they would ask, politely giving the clock this title of honor, just as Champlain had given it to a few of their great chiefs.

The Frenchman answered: "When he strikes twelve, he says, 'Hang on the kettle—*Sagamité* will soon be hot.' When he strikes four, he says, 'Time to get up and go home!'"

The visitors obeyed both commands. They would stay to dinner but at four they would leave and the missionaries would have peace.

One day Savignon came to listen to the clock.

"Did I not tell you so?" he asked the Indian visitors. "It speaks just like the one in Paris--France."

The Indians looked at Savignon with new respect. Some of them even wondered whether there was anything in that story about King Louis being pulled around by eight moose.

Almost as much as the clock the Indians liked Echon's magnifying glass. Through one lens a flea looked like a great monster. Another multiplied it so they could see eleven fleas instead of one. This was less popular, the Indians perhaps feeling that they had enough fleas already.

Tom sympathized with this point of view. He was glad to be out on the lakes again.

Still he did not find the great river. The early frosts found him traveling along the southern shore of Lake Erie. For the first time he heard the voice of Niagara Falls. His Indian friends had told him only that it was larger than other falls. He ought to see it, they said, and tell his master about it. Now, as he stood in awe gazing up at that moving mountain of water, he knew that he could never find words for it. Its power and majesty must be seen to be believed.

He was back at Captain Darontal's village early in December. With Darontal and other men from the village, they went to Ihonatiria at Christmas time. The Indians loved the Christmas ceremonies. They stayed and saw the Pageant of the Three Kings on the sixth of January.

"I must tell my master about it some day," Tom said.

CHAPTER 17

CHRISTMAS EVE

Tom did not go to the trading fair at Quebec in 1635. He sent word by Darontal that he would go west in search of the river early in the spring and come to Quebec with a report of his explorations in the early winter.

So his journey to Quebec that year was made not in a canoe but on snowshoes with a toboggan across frozen rivers, down hills shining with icy crust, under pines more white than green, around falls where the water still moved under columns of ice.

He lived on *sagamité* made with cornmeal and smoked fish. He slept on the toboggan on and under robes of beaver. Usually he shaved his beard as a courtesy to his Indian friends, who considered even Champlain's beard ugly. For this winter journey Tom had let his grow. It kept his chin and cheeks from freezing as he faced the north winds. There was often ice on it when he woke in the mornings.

He kept track of the days by making scratches on the frame of one of his snowshoes, but he was not sure, as he passed the rapids of La Chine, whether he had missed a day or two. He had hoped to reach Quebec well before Christmas. He wanted to hear mass on Christmas Day.

It took a long time to get past the rapids. He had to go by land. The river was frozen in places but the boiling whirlpools cracked the ice and set cakes grinding against each other. Below the falls the water was solidly frozen and he was able to follow the river for some distance. Later, when the tide began to meet the river current, he had to take to the land again. Now he began to see familiar landmarks. At last, one afternoon at sunset, he saw the light strike on something blue and white against the sky and he knew that he was looking on the flag at the fort.

He hurried towards it in the twilight. The sky was never completely dark because, as the red glow of sunset faded, the northern lights flashed across the sky in flags of shining white, then arched in quivering bands of green and rose color. Suddenly they were like great red flames and the snow all around him turned a deep glowing pink.

He left those fiery meadows and followed a familiar trail towards the fort through the woods. There was an open place, he remembered, in the woods where deer often gathered in the winter. When he reached it, the snow was shining pink there too. On the edge of it he saw an Indian kneeling in the snow.

Tom recognized him and spoke to him in Montagnais.

"It is a cold night to kneel in the snow, my brother," he said.

"Speak quietly, Tom Lee," the Indian said almost in a whisper. "This is the evening before Christ's birthday. The Black Robes"— he meant the Jesuits—"have told me that on that evening all the animals kneel down waiting for the Christ Child to come. I am watching for a deer to kneel down too."

Tom left him still kneeling there, and hurried to the fort. So he had really missed two days and this was Christmas Eve.

"You are in time," said the soldier who greeted him. "You will find him awake. He has asked for you."

"Is my master ill?"

Champlain, the soldier told Tom, had been ill and partly paralyzed since last October.

One of the priests met him in the dining hall and, like the soldier, said, "You are in time. He will be happy to see you. Go in."

In the Governor's chamber, from which he could see the frozen river, Champlain was propped up on pillows on his hard narrow bed. He looked very thin and white in the glow of the lighted candles, but the smile he gave when he saw Tom in the doorway made his face shine as if many more candles had been lighted there.

"Thomas—I knew you would come," he said.

Tom knelt by the bed. Champlain put his hand for a moment on his servant's head. Neither spoke of his illness.

"Why," Champlain said at last, "you have a beard! Like a Frenchman! I thought you were too much of an Indian for that. Come now, have you maps to show me? Tell me quickly what you have seen. We shall be interrupted. The children are coming in soon to sing their carol. Have you found the river—the Mississippi?"

"Yes," Tom said smiling down at him and holding out the map, "I have found the river."

He had marked on the map the route he had followed that summer and Champlain followed with a thin finger his course along the shores of Lake Michigan. Then a long portage, a maze of small streams, more portages, lakes, ponds. Then a river. At last The River.

"I could not go all the way down it," Tom said. "It became so large and rushed so fast that I knew it was too strong for me. I could find no guides to go farther. It was a hard and long enough journey as it was for me to get back upstream. But it is the river and it may lead to the Pacific side of the isthmus you told me about so long ago. The one you wanted to have a canal cut across. Only," he said honestly, "I think it is more likely it comes out east of the isthmus."

Color flushed Champlain's thin cheeks.

"In any case," he said, "wherever it runs, what a Christmas gift you have brought me. And what an empire for France."

He studied the map in silence for a few moments. Then he said, "And there is a present for you in that chest there, Thomas. Lift up the lid."

Tom opened the chest. He saw scarlet silk, birds, flowers, butterflies.

"A robe!" he said. "A Chinese robe!"

"Yes," said Champlain. "Like Nicolet's. Take it with you, Thomas. Wear it when you reach Cathay. Put it on now—let me see how you look in it."

So Tom slipped the scarlet robe with the threads of gold and brilliant colors, its loops and buttons of scarlet cord, over his shoulders. He was still wearing it when they heard the footsteps of the Indian children crossing the hall.

They stood, a dozen of them, just outside Champlain's door where he could see them. They were neatly dressed in French

cassocks with clean white surplices. Their black eyes sparkled in the candlelight. The priest lifted his hand and they began to sing.

> *"Aske ek watatennonten shekwachiendaen*
> *Iontonk ontatiende..."*

Tom watched his master while the singing went on until the last notes of the carol died away. He thought he had never seen such a look of happiness on his face—on any face.

"Translate for me, please, Thomas," Champlain said and for the last time Tom acted as his interpreter.

"The title," he said, "is Jesous Ahatonia. It means Jesus is born. The first verse says, '*Listen to what the angels say. Do not refuse to hear their message. The Divine Child is born today, son of the Virgin Mary. Let us adore him! Jesus is born!*'"

"I remember the carol. I sang it when I was a boy in Brouage," Champlain said when the singing was over. "Thank you, Thomas. There are presents for the children there. Will you give them to me?"

Tom brought them to him. They were rosaries of bright beads. Champlain handed one to each child, saying, "Jesus is born," and the Indians bowed their thanks, repeating, "Jesous Ahatonia."

Soon they had all gone and the room was quiet again. Tom sat on a stool beside the bed and told his master how he had heard the carol sung before in Ihonatiria.

"Father Brébeuf wrote it," he said. "They sang it at the Pageant of the Three Kings last winter."

"Tell me about it," Champlain said.

So Tom told how the priests had sent the Huron boys and girls to get materials to make a grotto for the Christ Child.

"One little girl," he said, "brought sweet grass to line the bed for the infant Jesus. The carved figures of the Virgin and Joseph and the kneeling animals were set up around the manger. There was midnight mass and many Indians came and knelt at the grotto. Then came the Three Kings. Each wore a coronet of eagle feathers and had a scepter trimmed with *matachias*. Their robes were of beaver. One little fat one kept tripping over his, it was so long and grand. Each King had a company of his friends behind him, all dressed in their best.

"The first company started marching towards the grotto at the sound of a trumpet. They carried a star and a sky-blue flag. The second company met them, asked where they were going and joined them. The third did the same. They marched into the church and laid their scepters and presents of shell beads at the feet of Jesus."

"You make me see it," Champlain said. "You have long been my ears and my tongue. Now you are my eyes too."

He slept for some time after that. Tom sat beside him. At times his master's breathing almost seemed to fade away. Just before midnight he woke and listened to the music coming from the church of Our Lady of the Recovery. As the clock began to strike, the cannon boomed for the Te Deum.

Champlain smiled.

"Do you remember the last time you heard them?" he asked.

Tom nodded. He would never forget the grief he had felt when he heard the guns from the fort salute the English ships, when he had paddled away knowing that Etienne and Nicholas had betrayed Quebec and Champlain.

"God's victory this time," Champlain said.

They were the last words Tom heard him speak. He died the next day, so quietly that the priest who was with him hardly knew when his breathing stopped.

Amid the common grief of French and Indians, he was buried with what ceremony the little settlement on the edge of the wilderness could use. A chapel was built for his tomb. He left his property to the church of Our Lady of the Recovery. His dream of a city on the rock with shining towers came true. French is still heard in its streets. The lilies of France are still displayed beside the English flag. The great cathedral of Quebec now stands near the site of the first small church.

And his servant Thomas? Did he follow the Mississippi to the Gulf and cross the isthmus to the Pacific? Did he find his way to the Orient and wear his scarlet robe at the court of the Great Khan?

Perhaps. No one knows.

In 1867 a fourteen-year-old boy named Lee tugged at a piece of metal, half buried in the mud near Muskrat Lake, New York, and found himself holding an astrolabe, dated 1603. It was near where Champlain lost his in 1613. Was it his? And was its finder a many times great-grandson of Tom Lee?

Again, no one knows, for, like the other men who helped make a wilderness into a great country, Thomas Godfrey Lee is just one of many shadows in that wilderness. We can be sure only of one thing. Wherever he went—down muddy rivers, across blue mountain ranges, up torrents of white water, through green swamps, over blinding snow fields, he carried with him the spirit of a great man, his master—Samuel de Champlain, gentleman.

9 781922 919021